BAD DOG
GOOD WOLF

by
ERIC LITTLE

CHAPTER ONE

Awake

I awakened to the taste of blood in my mouth, and it wasn't mine.

I licked my lips and tried to pierce the fog, where I was pretty sure memories were supposed to go. I felt strange, as if my body had grown larger. I didn't know where I was or how I got there. I was standing on all fours, the muscles in my arms rippling powerfully. A faint sheen of sweat rolled down my head and tangled hair. I studied my arms and found something looked very wrong with my hands. I felt intensely alive but confused.

"Dog Three! Down! Bad dog! Down now!" an angry man shouted at me. I felt a compulsion to fall into a crouch on the ground that was visceral and almost overpowering, but I resisted. I didn't know what was going on, and why I felt such an intense need to obey.

I looked around, and there were others stretched on the ground, paws in front of them. Their gazes focused on the angry man—he was evil, I knew in my gut. One of them glanced at me and whined. The bad man did something with the Shiny—an object in his hand, and my pack mate convulsed in pain. Returning my gaze to the bad man, I growled, "You're the bad dog!" softly as I lowered myself into the good-dog position. It was not quick enough.

When I came to again, I was curled up in a ball, my muscles knotted with pain. I was trembling slightly but pretended to still be asleep. The others of my pack were still in good-dog position, and I counted them: twelve. I watched from slit eyes, carefully listening to the bad man. He and his pack all dressed alike. I lost count at twenty-five.

They were gathered around a wire thing with two wheels. There was a body on the ground, and I almost growled, but stopped myself. A memory began to play in my head.

"Enemy," the commander had said over and over, as he showed us vids." Enemy! Kill the Enemy!" Then he tested us. It was very bad to fail. We learned to obey quickly or not at all. Only half of us survived.

Not a good memory, but I felt my *self* swell inside as my thoughts grew clearer.

I remembered.

I used to be a Marine. I used to be human—but now I am a dog.

Dog Three.

Anger rumbled inside me.

"The Dogs caught the spy while he was still in Zone A-Six. Dog Three tore his throat out in mid-air while he was riding that," the Sailor said to the bad man, pointing at the wire thing, but staring at me.

"Those beasts are damned frightening, but I guess that's what we need to guard the Special Weapons magazine. Still, I have nightmares about your controller failing one day. Hope you keep plenty of backups." Then the Sailor saluted. I remembered doing that, saluting.

I felt a sense of loss.

"The controller is unnecessary now. The Dogs are fully conditioned. I simply use this to reinforce orders. The important thing is that we need to remind the damn wolves who's alpha on a regular basis," the bad man said. His words lit a fire in my brain.

Wolves. I seized hold of the word and in my mind an image of a fierce predator congealed around it. *We are Wolves! Not Dogs!* I realized.

They had lied.

I bared my teeth unconsciously. One of the human pack began trembling and pointing at me. The bad man everyone was calling Commander turned to face me.

The next time I woke up, we were in our quarters. My head hurt, but I was gently nestled in a pile of Dogs—no, Wolves. Almost everyone else was sleeping. I felt warm and loved. I thought about what I had discovered. I had been a Marine, a man like the Commander's pack. But they had made me a Dog. A slave- Dog they turned into a killer. Now I was awake. Now I knew. I wasn't their Marine anymore and they were bad when they made me a Dog. We weren't slave-Dogs. We weren't bad killers. I nuzzled my way deeper into the pile of sleeping Wolves. The others would remember too. Maybe not right away, but my pack were all going to wake up. I would make sure of it.

Then I fell back asleep, and my head didn't hurt anymore.

In the morning, I told the others the truth.

"We are Wolves."

At first, they looked away and ignored me. But I was the alpha of this pack. My body settled into a coiled spring, ready to rend and tear. A very low rumble came out of my chest. They all dropped to good-dog position immediately.

We are now of one mind. We are pack, my pack.

3

"We have to get out of here. We need to go somewhere where they can't hurt us," I said.

My pack liked that. A lot of tail thumping floor. I tried to think about what came next as my pack watched me, waiting for the answer, even if I didn't exactly know the question. That came first.

Dogs belong to people. Wolves are free. We are Wolves, so... we need to be free, I thought. How do we do that? Suddenly, a rush of exhilaration washed over me. A plan was what we needed. I abruptly understood that not only did I remember fragments of being a Marine, I remembered planning an attack on someone I couldn't quite picture. I could do this!

"I have a plan. We aren't Dogs. We were humans, part of their pack and they changed us. They cast us out and made us killers, but we are more. We are not humans' slaves, we are WOLVES!" I announced. It got kind of noisy for a moment, yelps and howls mostly. Then our night keeper "Sleepy" banged on the bars of our cage and it quieted down quickly. Sleepy had a Shiny in his hand too, and nobody wanted that.

When it was time for patrol, we pretended to be good Dogs.

Our day keeper, "Stinky", lagged behind to sneak a smoke, like he usually did. He was tall and lean, and easily distracted. This was the chance I had been looking for. I quickly sent Dog Eleven and Dog Six to scout ahead, to warn us if humans approached. The rest of my pack slipped through the forest silently, heading to a forest hollow we had passed some days ago.

All day, I had been wondering if I could still walk upright like the human I used to be.

Everyone stopped to watch as I pushed off my forelegs. I didn't push hard enough, and only went partly vertical for a moment. The second time worked better, if a bit wobbly at first.

Standing upright hurt, but I ignored it. After a bit, I tottered forward on my haunches. Then things shifted into position, and it only hurt a little. I took another step and my pack barked in excitement. I hushed them and took a third step. Then another. Lots of tail wagging. Soon, some of the others were trying to stand erect as well. It was very exciting.

"We can do this," I said as I returned to dog posture. "Practice more later." The forest air had begun to reek of Stinky's presence. We had shifted back to the normal Zone A-Six patrol patterns by the time he joined us. Our keeper stunk of rancid smoke, and I wondered how the humans could ignore such nasty smells. I shook my head, and my wild tangled mane shifted out of the way. We followed him to the Zone A-Six exit, where Stinky's hand danced across a small blinking pad. I watched very carefully.

I can do that, I thought, looking down at my paws.

They were very big, with wide razor talons jutting out of each stubby finger. I experimentally moved my thumb back and forth, then curled my paw into a fist. Stinky was oblivious, sure that we were all good Dogs. I suddenly remembered the feeling of hitting something with my fist and feeling powerful and wondered if I was still powerful. Flashing my fist out into a thick tree branch, I broke it and it splintered, falling noisily. *Yes*, I thought, *I am stronger than I've ever been*. Leaning into the shadow of a fir next to the gate, where Stinky couldn't see me, I smiled.

That night I practiced stretching out the toes on my forepaws, retracting my claws and tapping on the floor—like Stinky when he clicked on the pad that opened our gate. It took longer than I expected.

By breakfast the next day all of us had practiced walking upright, and were able to loosely simulate a human's walk, at least from a distance. That morning, instead of everyone rushing the troughs and gobbling down gruel as fast as possible, I controlled access so that everyone got a fair share, and plenty of time to eat it.

"We are pack, and selfish behavior is beneath us," I said. Tails wagged, even though we were Wolves and not Dogs.

"We cannot fight the endless ranks of our enemy," I said to growls of acknowledgement. "But we can leave this place and find sanctuary someplace where we don't have to be Dogs anymore. We are Wolves! We are pack! We are greater than we know! We fight smart, not dumb," I explained.

Lots of tail wagging.

"This afternoon when we patrol Zone A-Six, we will spread out and find some of those false skins the humans drape themselves with—they call them 'clothing'. We will need them to slip by the sailors without being noticed. We don't want the humans to see us or they'll stop us," I explained. "We can't kill any of them or all the remaining sailors will converge on us with overwhelming force," I explained.

Not many tails beat the floor at that. I sighed.

"Soon, we will be ready to run away," I said. They liked that a lot. *Keep it simple*, I reminded myself.

That night we washed the clothing we'd stolen from Stinky and his packmates. Humans didn't pay much attention to dirty clothing, but Wolves have a very good sense of smell. Even after washing in the sink, we all knew which pieces were Stinky's. We hid the clothing behind the Navy latrines they had trained us to use and clean. At the next patrol, we stuffed them into a hollow tree, so they'd be ready.

The only thing left to overcome was the Shiny in the commander's hand. Somehow it hurt us through our dog collars. We needed to get rid of the collars so the bad man's sailors couldn't hurt us when we ran away. The only time they were removed was when the humans sprayed us with hot water and soap.

Nobody liked bath time.

The next night after patrol was our weekly bath session. We carefully studied how the sailors removed our collars before hosing us down, and how they put them back on when we were dry. The humans were very careful, and lots of sailors stood by, ready to kill us if we turned on them.

We saw the trick catch at the back of our collars.

Nobody got much sleep that night as we fumbled, tried, and finally figured out how to open the dog collars ourselves. Once they were all off, I made everyone put the collars back on. Dog Five challenged me but backed down at the last moment. I was alpha.

"I have a plan," I snarled as he cowered before me, submitting.

Every day we practiced walking on hindlegs like humans. Then the day arrived when our chance to run away came.

It all started when we were on afternoon patrol in Forest Zone B-One and reports of an enemy breaking through in Zone B-Five got all kind of attention. We stopped, and I approached Stinky, who was sucking down gray smoke with a devotion we all found mystifying.

"Ahh, bug off! I'll catch up when I'm ready," demanded our keeper.

I pretended to be a good-Dog and backed away with my head down. When we were out of his sight in the forest, we ran to the place where we had stashed the clothes and took off each other's dog collars and put them in a little pile. Then everyone peed on them.

"Dog Four, Dog Seven—spread out a little more. When we reach the gate, we'll be wearing clothing and walking upright like humans. We don't know if any sailors are actively watching, so assume they are," I ordered. I added, "This will work; soon we'll be free!" as I turned to tap out the sequence I'd seen the keeper enter day after day. It only took two tries to get it right, and the gate clicked open. I nodded to my pack.

It was a good thing that no one turned out to be watching, because we weren't very good at appearing human—not yet. As each of us shuffled through the gate, we were odd-looking, uncomfortable in human clothing. We didn't understand how to wear it like the humans yet. We were also sporting a lot more hair than any naked ape ever had. My pack still found a measure of grace somewhere in all that, and this made me proud.

I closed the gate behind us. Then we fell to all fours and ran like hell.

But it's never as simple as you think it's going to be.

The next two gates were no problem, but then we got to the edge of the woods. We had to cross a black road, get past a fence topped with concertina-wire-topped fence, and cross another road, before we could reach the cover of mesquite, aspen, and fir.

Open spaces were not safe. I knew that somehow.

"We're going to have to move fast but hold on to your clothing. These are the last barriers between us and freedom. Cut the fence. Go!" I ordered my pack. Talons sliced through the heavy wire fence, as if it were made of butter. The Commander was going to pick up our trail here, but there was no alternative. I crossed last, just in time to evade a growling metal monster with shining eyes, tearing down the inside road faster than any wolf could run.

It was terrifying, but we are Wolves and equal to any monster. I said so. Lots of growling and wagging. Then the four-wheeled metal monster came rushing back with friends and began spitting bullets. Three of my pack fell. We dragged them backward through the brush, until we reached the sea.

The sea reeked of salt, rotting fish and seaweed, and it was glorious. My pack licked the injured, cleaning their wounds. The bullets were pushed slowly back out of their flesh to fall into obscurity in the sand. We heal very quickly, if we're not actually killed.

I sent four Dogs out, two in each direction of the shoreline. I knew we had to move swiftly, now that the sailors had caught our scent. The punishment would be terrible if they caught us. I automatically cowered for a moment, as I thought about what they do to bad Dogs.

Then I remembered we are Wolves, not Dogs.

"We are Wolves! We are free and will not be called Dogs again! I am Three, never again Dog Three!" I declared. My pack yipped in excitement.

Six and Eleven returned to describe a high bridge spanning the water to another place. The bridge was right by the main gate to the base, and sailors were everywhere. That wasn't good. Thirteen and Five came back with better news of another island to the east.

It was low tide, and we found it easy to bypass the sailors in the muddy ground between us and the new island. They never left the dry pavement, and all their lights blinded them to the dark details of the tidal flats. *The black roads are bad*, I decided, and we turned right when the road turned left. We kept to the shoreline, chasing each other through the surf and feeling free for the first time any of us could remember. We worked our way east and then north along the beach. Our prints and scent were washed away behind us, concealing our trail.

Dawn found us at the base of a cliff, with empty beach stretching out in both directions. The newborn sun reflected across the water in a gleaming path that I wanted to walk, but I just got wet when I tried. In spite of the softness of the dry sand, the shelter of a grotto of trees and brush against the cliff, I knew we couldn't stay here. We were surrounded by water we couldn't drink without throwing up. We were thirsty.

Then Six found the stairs.

The stairs were quite unlike anything I could remember seeing. They were a haphazard blend of driftwood and weathered pine, with rope and old wooden ladders for safety rails. Some steps were broken, but we easily stepped over them. It was a long way up.

I pulled myself up over the top of the cliff and crouched on the small boardwalk leading into the forest. I could smell water and directed Five and Eleven to scout forward and to our left. To our right, I saw a puny chain-link fence that couldn't keep a cat in. Suddenly an old German Shepard came running noisily up to the other side of the fence, barking as he probably had a thousand times before. I lowered my head close to the fence and growled. The dog yelped once and rolled over on his back to present his throat. He was trembling.

I felt ashamed.

I know what it is to be a caged dog.

Slicing an opening in his fence before turning my back, I moved up the trail to a seldom traveled dirt road. I didn't look back to see if the dog seized the moment and claimed his freedom.

Five and Eleven found a freshwater bog hidden in a remote forest clearing. We heard the frogs singing as we drew near. The water was clear and fresh, with a vibrant character I can't ever remember tasting before. But then again, there's not a lot I do remember. We drank our fill and washed the salt from our fur and clothes. Then we found a sunny spot and air dried. Several small flying monsters buzzed by overhead, never coming close to spotting us.

Shelter, then food, I decided.

Dividing up into teams and scouting outward, we found four houses, three of them inhabited. Nine found the prize: an ancient barn so covered with blackberry vines and saplings that it was completely concealed; unless you happen to run your nose into the side of it, which is how Nine found it. Once inside the wide structure we found a generous open space that was empty, except for some kind of bench with a detachable bar and heavy metal wheels on the ends. There was also a decrepit four-wheeled monster tucked away in a corner. It made a convenient stair to the upper floor of the barn, where someone apparently kept bundles of dried grass. I tore one open and spread it on the floor, before finally sitting down. It was soft. Enough light filtered in for everyone to comfortably see around them. The pack followed my example and were soon collapsing in delight on their straw beds.

"I smell many deer here. Two, Ten, Four and Seven, go west, deeper into the forest. One, Five, Eight and Twelve, go south along the cliff's edge, then turn inland paralleling the other party. Stealth mode everyone! Take down the prey and bring it back here before dark. Go!" I ordered from the comfort of my grass pillow.

Then I rose to four feet and trotted down and out the new blackberry tunnel. I quietly made my way through the undergrowth to the nearest house. Six, Nine, and Eleven fell into place at my back. Thirteen remained behind to guard the den.

It was an odd place, surrounded on all sides by a forest glade, bright with sunlight. Beyond that were incense cedar, mountain hemlock and silver fir. That was where we were

11

hiding. The forest was a wall of verdant green. The yellow building was like two houses sitting on top of each other. The bottom one had a round, wrinkly human who was surrounded by cats. I crinkled my nose and turned my attention to the wooden dwelling on top. It was empty but smelled of human male and wine. We crossed the little-used dirt road and situated ourselves in the sun-drenched bushes and grasses across from Cat-lady's big window. Our eyesight and hearing are very good. She was watching a vid about burning things and eating them. Why would anyone want to do that? It was fascinating. We fell into a trance of sorts, one that only broke when the sun slid west, bathing us in shadow. I immediately withdrew and returned to our base, the former barn.

Dinner was waiting. We didn't burn it first.

That night, the male returned to his house in the trees and started burning things, like in the show. The smells that wafted our way were intriguing and made my mouth water in spite of my full stomach. This made me realize I had always been hungry when I had been a Dog. This rich venison gave me enough of what I needed for the first time in as long as I could remember.

I fell asleep that evening in a pile of Wolves, warm and full-bellied, safe in our hidden den.

It was a good day.

CHAPTER 2

Lumberjacks & Schick Razors

The next day I tried to stay away, but wrinkly Cat-lady's vids were mesmerizing. This morning, most of us were lying comfortably hidden in the underbrush, intently watching food shows through the window over the old lady's right shoulder. This show was about burning perfectly good meat slowly. Eight's stomach rumbled and Eleven nipped him. Everyone burst out in silent wolf laughs.

The shaving mini-shows intrigued me. When humans want to get rid of hair, they smear white stuff over it and scrape it off with something like sticks. That could be helpful when we needed to pretend we were humans! I was under no illusion that we wouldn't need every advantage we could find to continue avoiding the Commander and his sailors. Luckily, this island was thinly populated with humans, and no Wolves—at least until now.

The next morning, Wine-guy came down the exterior stairs as usual and got into a small metal contraption that didn't spit bullets and roared away. I eased back from the bushes and loped around the wrinkly one's cat haven to the backyard, where I leapt up to seize the roof's edge and pulled myself up. I walked along the top of the roof to the back of Wine-guy's house in the trees. A window was cracked open, so I slipped in, and immediately opened the door to the balcony so the others could join me in exploring. Everyone bumped their heads against the ceiling at least once. I didn't realize how much larger we were than humans until I entered one of their dens.

In his latrine, there was a little sink and a funny cell just large enough to squeeze into. It had plastic curtains unsuccessfully hiding it. Seven discovered a metal stick on the inside that rotated. When she turned it, it drenched her in cold water which was quite a surprise. In a tiny cabinet we found a can of the white stuff and the hair-scraper sticks called Schick razors. We wet my head in the cell and smeared the white stuff all over my head, except my face below the nose. Then, Six and Twelve scraped off all my hair. It was harder than it looked in the mini-shows, and it's a very good thing we heal so rapidly.

When they finished, I stood up as fully as I could, considering the ceiling. Walking upright was getting easier now that I had some practice. Then I stepped over to the mirror to study the stranger in it. I looked almost human. I sort of looked like those guys that wrestle trees into chunks and run on wet logs without falling in. I didn't get to see much because the wrinkly one changed the channel. *Lumberjacks*, I think they're called. Maybe we could pass as lumberjacks when we had to interact with humans? By the time it started getting dark, we had shaved everyone else's heads too. It took a while to clean up after ourselves, but we had been trained to clean our quarters to military standards. Seven even cleaned the toilet out of habit.

The ripe venison was even more tender the second night, but we were going to have to hunt again the next day. That was okay, from the scent and scat, deer vastly outnumbered the humans on this island. Besides, hunting deer in the forest was what Wolves did. I was pretty sure we excelled at it.

That night there was a full moon, which drew our gazes like a magnet. We wanted to sing like we usually did, but I ordered everyone to stay silent. The Commander was still out there, and he wasn't going to give up the hunt. He didn't need any clues from us. We all knew he would find us eventually—we were still too close for safety. I worried some but didn't share my thoughts.

The next morning found all of us hidden in the bushes, again, watching the vids through the downstairs window. One of the mini-shows depicted powerfully built humans laying on a bench pushing a bar up and down, like the one we found in the barn, with wheels on the ends. The humans were very happy and strong after doing this. Their little teeth were very white, but nobody got scared when they showed them to everyone.

"They seem more powerful than the humans we've encountered since we escaped. We should try that; maybe we'll get stronger, too," I suggested, once the main show had resumed. This one was about two hungry humans in the woods looking for food and shelter. It was very instructive, especially the part about starting fires to burn their food.

One of the humans was always barefoot. I looked down at my feet. They seemed stubby in comparison to his. We all watched in fascination until Cat-lady changed the channel to something with humans jumping around to thumping sounds.

The next morning, we climbed up to Wine-guy's house and let ourselves in the bedroom window again. Twelve startled us when he sat on a black stick while getting comfortable in the black leather chair and the vids turned on. It only took a moment for us to figure out how to change the shows. Lots of tail wagging over that one. I claimed the big leather chair in front of the vids as was my right as alpha, but

I let Seven wield the changing stick. She was much better at the tech stuff.

There were so many choices to watch, but we ended up with the one called "Alaskan Loggers" several times. We all studied the humans, who were quite hairy and strong, but talked funny. I noticed that the loggers had very little fur on their arms and hands, so that was the next thing we shaved. Then we cleaned up, mopped the floors, and let ourselves out the way we came in.

We chased down another three fat deer that evening, so everyone had plenty to eat. Wine-guy came home after sundown, he didn't start burning food right away, but came back out on the balcony and peered into the dark as if looking for something. After a minute he shook his head and returned to start burning his dinner. It smelled good, despite what he did to it.

CHAPTER 3

Mongol Heavy Metal

That night I dreamed I was human and had a mate and two pups. I was very happy because I was coming back from the war on leave, but my house was empty when I got there. My mate had left a note saying she was tired of being alone and had found a new love and father for our children. Someone who would actually be there when she wanted him. I was filled with sadness and looked everywhere but couldn't find any sign of them. Then I awoke with a wet face and realized I was surrounded by a loving pile of Wolves. There was no reason to feel lonely, not anymore. I Wolf-smiled, snuggled deeper into the mound and let sleep carry me away to a kinder, gentler night.

We began lifting the wheel-bar and practicing walking upright again the next day. The wheels were too light so Two figured out how to add the other metal pieces. It was still easy, so we practiced doing it very fast. My arms were sore for the first time I could remember, but the walking was easier.

"We need better clothes to pass for human," I said. We searched the empty house at the end of the dirt road and found some long coats and muddy plastic shoes, as well as a big box of floppy wool hats. Everyone immediately put hats on their bald heads and took turns admiring themselves in the bathroom mirror. All those Wolves trying to use the mirror in the tiny latrine was one of the reasons I loved being a pack—everyone dutifully follows the pack hierarchy, patiently waiting their turn. There was no shoving or crowding.

Twelve noticed that our arms were bigger, something we would never have noticed had they still been covered in fur. We doubled our exercises.

Back at the house in the trees, in the back of his closet, Wine-guy had many shirts and a few black pants big enough to fit us. They smelled like no one had worn them in years. We took them. The big discovery was in the Cat-lady's attic; boxes full of mothball-smelling colorful sweaters. The females of the pack seemed to like them. I thought they were ugly, but they did make our females look more human – human female, specifically. Then we cleaned his kitchen and dusted his thousands of books in the big room in exchange.

Later, watching vids, we discovered something called YouTube, a massive place where you could find out about anything.

There was Mongol heavy metal music, which we liked, and vids on how to repair metal monsters, which were useless. There were fighting vids and food burning shows. We found that there were many things of interest to Wolves, as well. There were even hunting clips! Eleven, Seven, and Eight soon taught themselves to read, then began to teach the rest of us.

Six and Twelve studied how to select clothing that would help us blend in with the human herd. It turned out that there were differences that told you how old, or successful you were just by the clothing! The big surprise was finding out that many of the female's sweaters had stylized designs of cats on them. Eleven just looked away and said that meant cats should watch out. I wouldn't want to wear them, but then I didn't really get the whole idea of wearing false skins when it was warm outside anyway.

We also found some new ways to lift the metal wheel-bar so we could strengthen our flanks—which the vids called 'cores'. After only a few days, it made it easier to walk upright for longer periods of time.

Our minds were like sponges, aching to fill all the holes where memories used to go. And learning connected with old threads of who we had once been. We were getting stronger and smarter by the day. This was imperative; our very survival depended on it. We were far too close to the Naval base on Indian Island. And the world was a lot bigger place than any of us remembered.

We began carving out escape routes, because this beautiful haven couldn't be our home for long. We needed a territory that was safe for a Wolf to stop pretending to be human. One with lots of deer, a place where Wolves outnumbered the humans.

A Wolf homeland.

Wine-guy had an old computer in the back of his closet that we found when sorting clothes for the wash. (We wondered why he didn't bring home Tide, which gets all the stains out.) YouTube showed us what it was—a computer—and how to refurbish it. YouTube also showed us how to use it.

The Wine-guy also had two other computers, which he used regularly. We never touched those.

We set up the refurbished computer in the hidden barn, where it was barely in Wi-Fi range. Once we all learned how to read and type, different wolves were using it all day long.

Then we discovered Google.

19

There was information about *everything* out there in cyberspace.

I wanted to know more about our enemy, so we began researching the Naval Magazine that we escaped from on Indian Island. I found out his name was Commander Elwha. If I could figure out where his den was, I could break his Shiny. Maybe kill him slowly and eat him. Opinions differed, and this was a popular subject as we regained verbal and reasoning skills daily.

Unfortunately, the internet turned out to be more complex than we realized, and we apparently set off alarms by treading in places we shouldn't have.

CHAPTER 4

Dog Hunt

We heard them coming just before true dawn.

The rumble of numerous heavy metal monsters entering our little dirt road almost a kilometer away caught our attention. It was accompanied by numerous small flying things like metal buzzards zooming through the tree-line up and down the eastern coast of our little island. They were looking for us and knew where to look. We knew they would find us someday and had dreaded it. Now that day had dawned.

Commander Elwha was coming.

They thought we were Dogs—and Dogs don't climb trees. But we were Wolves and we had sharp talons, powerful thighs, and could walk upright. We could climb anything we wanted.

And we were in a forest.

Leaping to my feet, I snarled to the pack.

"You know what to do!" They growled, nodding, all eyes fixed on me. "Get the clothes, help each other. Everything, including the floppy hats," I barked. They jumped to obey. "We gear up like humans," I murmured in a rumble, "and we outsmart them like Wolves."

My pack liked that.

Outside in the predawn, we flowed up into the forest canopy like a waterfall in reverse. We stopped thirty meters up and began following the signs we had carved into the trees to mark the way. We jumped from tree to tree, long leaps that humans couldn't manage and would never expect from Dogs. We were half a kilometer away by the time the ground forces arrived at the stacked house. The noise of confusion reigned from what we could hear.

The wrinkly Cat-lady and her tribe of cats were very angry.

Then I heard the bay of bloodhounds. Stopping on a broad limb, I leaned out slightly to mark my scent on the ground far below. *Let's see what the hounds make of that*, I thought.

Then I was bounding from tree to tree, covering a significant distance. In the branches, we were far enough above the metal buzzards that they didn't detect us. They were searching below, not above. Thirty-five meters up in the mid-canopy of the forest was a strangely beautiful place, so many bright shades of green with the occasional pillar of sunlight piercing the canopy in golden splendor. I hardly noticed it at the time, but in later times the memory was vivid.

We heard that the bloodhounds were getting very upset and their frantic barking and yelps soon faded in the distance as if they were running back to safety. I made a little hoot sound like a scared puppy and silent laughter drifted down the trees like snow in winter. Wolf humor.

Dark gray clouds began rolling in at an alarming speed, mirrored in the water to look twice their size. Perfect—a storm! We were at the northwest corner of the island near a kayak rental place. They had big canoes as well. Nestling into crooks in the tree trunks where the limbs branched out, we held still, all within sight of each other but not to anyone on the ground. We patiently waited for the storm to hit and reduce visibility.

When the tempest made landfall, it hit like a giant hammer up in the trees. The storm pushed off the water angrily and pummeled us roughly, but we were not cats, afraid of a little water. I could just see the lights of Port Townsend from my perch, despite the storm. It was going to be a lot worse once we hit the water.

When the wind began to lessen a bit, I spoke up.

"Four large canoes, just like we discussed. Slice the chain and take the canoes to the water's edge. Three or four to a boat. Let's get paddles," I said. As I fetched the paddles from the storage shed with some of my Wolves, I realized how snug it would be in the boats, but I savored this. One is never alone in the world when you're a Wolf. I briefly wondered if humans were lonely like I had been in that bad dream. Then I shook my head and raised the metal chain in my paw to slice the shed lock cleanly off. We were in.

"We need thirteen oars," I ordered. Some of us filled our arms, waddled to the boats and deposited them, several others lagged behind to shut the door to the shed and bend the chain links back into shape so it would kind of hold together. Once we were all accounted for, we shoved the boats into the violent surf. I jumped in last. Everyone was paddling hard as we broke through the waves into deeper water. All four canoes made it out there past the surf.

"Tomato mulch. Now!" I ordered. I don't know why the rolls of black fabric we found in the barn were called that, but they made very good camouflage during a storm. Everyone in the boats stretched out the cloth over their heads. It leaked pretty bad, but the metal buzzards never spotted us, so it must have worked.

It was late afternoon before we paddled up to the marina in Port Townsend and secured the boats to the dock. We were fully dressed human style, with large beards and pants loose enough to hide a tail, coats and even some "boots". We were also soaking wet.

I climbed the short ladder to the main dock and stood to the side as my pack joined me. The wind whipping off the water was already drying my clothes. I turned and began walking in the direction of the shore, my pack spread around me in a protective layer. When we passed by two slight humans, one mumbled, "Arrogant hipsters." I have no idea what arrogant hipsters are, but it couldn't be bad, because the humans kept walking the other direction.

"Boys, will you give me a hand, please?" asked an old male as we approached him. His small boat was being tugged out by the current, and he wasn't strong enough to pull it in. I nodded to him.

"Seven, Four, bring in the man's boat," I said. They not only pulled it in but lifted it out of the water and set it on the dock.

"Thank you! Thank you!" said the old human, pressing something into my paw as he shook it. I carefully squeezed back, then turned and continued down the dock.

After a moment, I looked in my hand and found two one-hundred-dollar bills. We'd studied this on YouTube. It was money, and you needed it for everything in this human-stuffed world. I stopped by a small booth that sold cups of something that smelled heavenly.

"Which way to the Whidbey Island ferry?" I asked the young female. She flashed her tiny teeth and pointed.

We were just in time.

CHAPTER 5

Pioneer Square

We walked forward on board the ferry to Whidbey Island, as self-absorbed humans streamed past us, always making sure to keep us at arm's length as though from a subconscious recognition of an alpha predator in the neighborhood. Ten found some metal stairs and we climbed up to the next deck. Fewer humans up there. Large, dark windows in front drew us like bears to honey. When we stepped out into glorious night, a scent-wind of hurricane proportions poured over us. The brine dominated, but the aromas of decaying sea life, the green smell of plankton night blooming, the musty-feathered gulls hanging in the air watching the dark water. The diesel of the ferry's engines, and the iron smell surrounded us. It was all shoved in our faces by the noisy sea wind, supercharging our already powerful sense of smell. We had wide Wolf grins as we thrust our noses into the wind and drank deeply of the sea of scent.

Another big ferry passed us going the other way, out in the cold waters of Puget Sound. Our tickets said we were supposed to get on the Puget Sound ferry once we docked at Coupeville and get off that one in old downtown Seattle. Ten said that this was as far as the two hundred-dollar bills would take us. I guess we were walking the rest of the way to the promised land, unless something else came up. That was okay, I found I liked getting a feel for someplace new as I was passing through; maybe replacing the missing memories in my head.

The lights of the docks grew in the dark, and I could feel the ferry's engines reverse.

"Back downstairs, time to go," I said to my pack.

We entered the flow of the human crowd at the exits; they gave way before us politely as we disembarked. We were thirteen standing Wolves noticeably out-bulking the humans and standing a little over two meters tall. Our powerful arms were a smidgen longer than the humans, our legs a little shorter and we were muscular in a way that was cut. We had big noses. We wore a hodgepodge of salvaged clothing that fit loose enough to hide our tails and pointy ears. All of our females wore ugly sweaters with cats on them.

We had no idea why people kept glancing our way.

When we listened, we found that we looked like jacked-up lumberjack hipsters run out of cheap beer. We had way too much hair, despite our shaved head and floppy hats. And where were our tattoos? We moved into the terminal with a coherent grace that only a pack is capable of, so maybe we were a hipster dance troop, or Delta force, whatever that is. It's amazing to me how humans talk in a crowd, as if they were alone and no one knew what they were saying. I think it's called gossip.

Wolves' ears are better than humans. We hear everything.

Two old males discussing the PS ferry to Seattle caught our attention; all we had to do was follow them. They kept speeding up for some reason. So, we sped up too. Each time. Then we were there. They looked tired, I thought.

We waited in line to show our tickets and then we followed the passengers onto the ferry. We immediately went upstairs to the deserted upper-deck and headed outside. A new flavor had crept into the wind's insistent push; mud and oil and small dead things. As our noses drank of the night my thoughts wandered and I found myself marveling at how far we'd come since I first woke up on Indian Island.

We had once been elite human Marines, then something happened. I couldn't really remember anything before Commander Elwha and his sailors trained us as captive, highly intelligent "Dogs". We had been fully capable of understanding complex instructions and maps. We guarded Navy Special Weapons and magazines for them and ran on all-fours all the time. We ate gruel in troughs like farm animals. Our masters controlled us by powerful collars around our thick furry necks that dispensed electro-shocks that could kill if allowed to go on too long. Usually they just produced burning agony and convulsions, followed by a welcome unconsciousness.

Now we are Wolves.

The map we'd memorized from Google indicated the best way to get back to the Olympic Peninsula and the Hoh rain forest would be to head south from Whidbey and cut across to Bainbridge Island, without going through any of the Commander's territory. We'd have to search for boats at the Seattle docks.

My pack poured out of the ferry street-level exit to form up around me. The crowd left noisily, as if anxious to get the hell out of there. We walked the deserted shining streets, our raised noses taking a good whiff of our surroundings. All eyes turned to me.

"Humans! What a wasteland," I declared as I eyed the crumbling brick street of the intersection. Four and five story buildings blocked out the sky around us, and you couldn't even see the stars. I nodded at Seven, who was becoming one of our best tech Wolves. Waking up was bringing back skills lost in time for all of us, and for her, computers were the specialty. She spoke fluent machine.

Twelve leaned closer and briefly fanned an impressive assortment of stolen wallets and cell phones. then bowed his head to me as alpha. We continued walking the wet streets of old Seattle. Twelve is a different kind of Wolf than most of us. He is a born thief, a sausage stealer who has regained lost skills at an amazing rate. He knows what the rules are, he just doesn't care. What he does care about is pack hierarchy and strength. Twelve feels that if you're not strong enough to hold on to something, then it's his to take, if he can. This is an acceptable, if not particularly tasteful, Wolf behavior, as long as he values pack. Sometimes you have to do underhanded things to survive and while all Wolves are capable of doing what it takes, some are downright gifted at it. Twelve is extraordinary, so it's good that he respects pack hierarchy.

We all watched Seven as she worked technical magic on the phone she got from Twelve. Her paws moved lightning fast; she didn't even have to think about stretching her digits.

"Wind is coming in off the water—that way is northwest," she said, pointing ahead. "We need to go west for three kilometers, then turn north until we see the water." Then she briefly bowed her head in respect, and I nodded back.

"Five and Eleven to me! Two, Seven, and Thirteen: cover our left. Eight, Ten, and Six: go right! Twelve and Nine: our rear. One and Four: scout out in front," I ordered.

Walking along the sidewalks of this ugly place, I looked around me. If this was the human's favorite city, I was not impressed. Sometimes I wondered if those mini-shows on TV were lying. Humans do that.

The mostly dark walls of the buildings were faded in patches of dull silver and blue from the occasional streetlight. Rusting four-wheeled metal carcasses cluttered the sides of the streets. Strips of dead soil hosted struggling bushes here and there, but only enough to make you realize what you were missing. Wolves are forest creatures, after all.

"Stay alert in this nose-deadening place—human predators could be anywhere. We don't want to attract attention by leaving any savaged bodies lying around," I said. Five drew in a breath, as if frightened, then dropped a silent Wolf laugh on us. I caught his eye and stared into them until he looked away, acknowledging my alpha status.

We continued on, into a desolate warehouse district, for five or six blocks without being noticed. Then we began smelling human smokers everywhere. We slowed down, mapping the hostiles by nose. They were trying to be quiet and probably thought they couldn't be detected. I snorted at their ineptitude. More silent Wolf laughs from my pack.

"Oh my! Hipsters! What's the matter, run out of PBR?" a rough voice asked from the shadow of an industrial canopy. The other humans chuckled. I smiled as well. Now we have confirmed the enemy's positions; Wolves have very good hearing.

"Looking for an authentic experience in old Seattle?" asked another from in front of us. Maybe he was supposed to startle us. This one smelled of sour sweat and gun oil and burnt herbs. He didn't notice Four and One slipping up behind him because he was busy watching his men sneak up behind us. We knew exactly where each one of them was the whole time, of course.

I began a low growl in my throat, then snarled the signal. Wolves exploded outward, taking down all enemy threats, and disarming the ones who gave up and bared neck. There weren't many of those. It was over very quickly. I looked to each Wolf, finding everyone unharmed.

29

"Drag the bodies into the shadows behind that building, and remove any weapons, food, or clothing we can use. Sentries out front while we salvage what we can from this," I ordered. Then I stepped over to the prisoners.

"Why do you hunt us?" I asked in a low, rumbling voice as I crouched to lower my head close to one of them. Slowly, I turned my oversized head to face him and flashed tooth. He screamed; a long desperate note followed by quick breathing.

"You looked like lost tourists! We was just going to rob you!" he explained in a staccato voice. Then he panted noisily and avoided my eyes. I leaned closer.

"Just rob?" I asked mildly, with a little growl at the end. The sudden odor of pungent ammonia permeated the nearby surroundings.

"Okay! Okay! We was going to have some fun with your ladies, but they'd be okay!" he babbled.

I wasn't the only one angered. Eleven's temperature was noticeably rising.

Most females would likely have been killed after this pack used them. I didn't know which offended me more— the out-of-heat forced mating, or the killing part. I winced my nose and nodded the pack's females over to my side. They had heard everything I had. I raised my chin at the enemy, and they all nodded, then fell to all fours.

It was up to them to decide the fate of those who would harm them.

First, they began slowly circling the would-be rapists and killers gathered on the ground in front of us. Then they began growling at such a low frequency that it reverberated in your thigh bones.

I turned my back on them and began walking down the sidewalk as before. The males fell back into formation around me, minus our females.

We knew they'd be along in a while.

At dawn, we moved underground. There was an entire underground city spread out along this way! Apparently once there was a big fire, and afterwards everyone just built the new city on top of the old burned one. No need to risk being seen in the full light of day. Commander Elwha and his sailors were still searching for us, but we weren't ready for them, not the way I wanted it to go down.

Unfortunately, it proved to be busier underground than I expected. Chains of tourists with powerful flashlights were led past our hiding spots in tour after tour. Every time we got started, another one came by! Guess everyone liked being down where it's warm and dark, but where's a Wolf pack to hide in the big city? We went back up to the streets and continued trotting down the gleaming streets in the dawns first blush.

Then we found it.

It was one of a hundred well-lit warehouses in this industrial section of the waterfront. The difference was that this one smelled exclusively of rotting fish, rat droppings, and moldy newspaper. It did not smell of humans, or anything with a pulse larger than a cat.

There were also no lights inside the windows. Just the exterior was lit with soulless spotlights and a forbidding locked gate. Maybe this was sufficient for deterring humans, but not Wolves. We were over the fence and at the building's exterior before humans would have been able to even detect our movement. Our wide, razor-sharp talons sunk into the dirty brick building's sides easily. We ran up the side of the building and onto the roof, where we regrouped and sucked in air through our nostrils to paint our surrounding in fat fragrance and sour note. We were alone.

Perfect.

There was a modest security shack isolated in the north corner of the tar roof. It was long empty, and relatively free of debris. We swabbed it out and laid down our sleeping bags in an irregular mattress. From here on the roof, we could cover the perimeter without being seen.

I gave the order to break out our new Licuado protein shakes, a well-balanced high calorie meal in a shaker. The mini-shows said it was optimal nutrition. While we found the shakes oddly lacking in flavor and texture, we were on the run, so fresh venison got moved to the back burner and Licuados must fuel the Wolf.

Five set three-hour watches, and the rest of us fell into a warm pile of Wolves, enjoying the close contact of our packmates as we drifted off. I fell into the dark of dream and saw things I tried not to remember when I woke up at dusk.

Just like every other night since I had become a Wolf.

CHAPTER 6

Shotguns & Kayaks

It was twilight. Up high here on the roof, in a small hut atop a deserted warehouse in old town Seattle we had a beautiful view of rose and orange hues as the glowing sun slipped out of sight. Dusk was abrupt, and soon it was full night.

"Wolves, please pile everything we looted off the enemy that attacked us last night, in the center of the room," I ordered. A heap of stuff materialized.

"Five, what do we have here?" I asked my second in command. He began picking each weapon up, expertly checking out each piece. He wore a confused look though, as he stared at his paws doing things he didn't remember knowing how to do.

"I think our paws remember Marine things!" I exclaimed excitedly. I waited impatiently while he worked through the pile, spending the time wondering what else our paws remembered. Then he lowered his head respectfully and began to report.

"Twelve pistols, mostly nine-millimeter; three fifty-caliber Desert Eagles; two forty-fives. Four shotguns, all twelve gauge, one of them a bullpup auto with extra magazines. Four Uzi's, five M16A2's, two M4's, and twenty-eight knives of various sizes," said Five as he began pawing through another pile.

Five is a good-looking Wolf still short of his prime. He is powerfully built with fog-grey fur and a white patch on his chest, not that it was visible under his human wardrobe. He has the patience of a cub, but I think he'll grow out of the arrogance of youth and become a great Wolf someday. I just wish he didn't think his path to alpha went straight through me. But the number two Wolf always wants to be number one. They can't help themselves.

However, I still had a Wolves' homeland to build and Five was just going to have to wait his turn. I turned my gaze back on Five and patiently waited. It didn't take long, people don't much care for silence, and are propelled to fill a vacuum with speech.

"Approximately twelve thousand dollars in cash, thirty-four credit cards, two small gold bars, and four pounds of assorted shiny jewelry. Eighteen long coats. Body armor for twenty fighters, but over half are too small to fit us. Thirty-two cell phones, and six smoke bombs," he finished. I nodded to him in appreciation, forgetting that it's probably not a good idea to let down my guard.

I thought about it. It seems we each remember only tiny bits and pieces of our past, but our paws remember all the instruments of violence. *What more are we capable that we didn't know about?* I wondered.

I turned my attention back to Eleven. She was the fastest and most agile among us, a Wolf of strength and femininity that I found quite attractive. I had already decided to be close by when she finally went into heat. Eleven would make a great mom, fierce and protective of her cubs. We would make beautiful Wolves together on that day I somehow knew.

I brought my attention back to the present.

"Eleven, distribute the guns. That bullpup has my name on it. Seven, cell phones and tablets. Twelve; you take responsibility for the money and shiny stuff. Don't screw it up. Nine, the clothing. One, the body armor! Thirteen, you are responsible for blades. Ten, all ammo. Two, food. Now!" I demanded.

Four minutes later, I had on torso armor with a long dusky purple coat, my new Benelli shotgun, a shiny fifty caliber pistol, a huge Bowie with a knuckle guard, and assorted throwing knives. I like throwing knives. You can never have too many.

My pack all checked each other's gear and traded a few things here and there to keep everyone as strapped up as possible. It's good to be pack. We are of one mind.

The night was dark, except for the few harsh cerulean streetlamps that were working. I missed the stars. The menacing clouds overhead began shedding rain that was someplace between a mist and a downpour. I felt cleaner but was glad I had my floppy hat. My shaved head felt the cold rain these days. I wasn't used to that.

We were watching a boat place from the roof of a nearby warehouse. The long dock was stuffed with every kind of boat imaginable. There were many other docks just like it. The wealth of choices was a little overwhelming for us. When we were Dogs there were no real choices. Then we found out we were actually Wolves and escaped. Hiding out on the island with the barn showed us a whole new world, one rich with choices. We thought that was all there was! We kept finding out the world is much bigger than we realized.

"How can we figure out which boats are best?" I thought furiously, trying to find a way to get my teeth into the problem and chew on it. Then I had it!

"Eleven, remember when we first discovered YouTube? In the beginning, humans jumping around to music was all we could find. Once we learned how to search the content, a whole world opened up—there were so many choices! We just need to repeat that learning process with the boats until we find the right ones for our needs," I said. Everyone got excited. Some tail wagging went down.

Eleven Wolf-grinned—she was happiest with a problem to chew on. I suddenly realized that I thought her smile was beautiful but pushed the thought way-down where I couldn't see it. Eleven was important to me in a way I didn't really understand.

I cleared my throat with a sub-woofer rumble. Now I had everyone's attention. I nodded minutely to Eleven, but of course all our pack saw it. Wolves notice these things. Eleven turned to face us.

"None of us were any good at reading back then, but after a little while, everyone realized that the scratches on the lower screen were alike when the humans jumped up and down to thumps. Then we found different scratches to show us other things. Once we figured out how to make our own marks, we were able to narrow the choices down!" Eleven declared happily. Lots of tails wagging at that. Everyone loved Eleven. And she was very smart.

"So the ships that are too big, we ignore. I think we are safer with four boats, same size as before. Five meters or less in length. That should narrow it down," suggested Ten. Ten was a quiet Wolf, one who made sure he was exactly where he was needed, at the proper times. But inside his head, Ten was an outside-the-box kind of Wolf, who sometimes saw things the rest of us missed. He never had much to say, but when he did speak everyone listened closely.

"We need enough oars, or those smelly machines that push the metal grendels around," said Seven. Grendels.

That's what she called the monsters. "I think I can make them go where we want," she added.

I had my doubts, but I trusted her. She is pack. And also very smart.

"Everyone take one side of a dock and look over the boats there," I said, "I'll take the third dock, left side." My Wolves leapt into action, happy to have a well-defined task.

But even with all those choices, we couldn't find a single large canoe, much less four of them. The only boats close enough to the water to paddle in were much too small. However, we did find something else. A whole lot of Kayaks! While on the island, we had all watched YouTube vids about kayaking, though we had never so much as physically touched one before. It seemed like a reasonable option, if we could manage it. I looked around for doubts but found none.

So I just smiled with all my teeth showing.

"Eight, do you have a sound suppressor on that carbine? Good! Please take out those two spotlights at the gate to the dock," I ordered. Two suppressed cracks cut the night in half. The dock entryway fell into darkness. We moved out under a crescent slice of moon, shining turquoise blue across the oily water.

"Move under the dock once you're in your kayak. We can practice moving around in there until we are ready. Don't whack your fellow Wolves over the head with your paddle, Eleven!" I said, too late.

It felt strange, stretching out my legs in a sitting position that was no doubt comfortable for a human. I, however, have a tail. It didn't help that I could barely squeeze into the largest size kayak we found. Half of us were in the water in our liberated kayaks, pushing the water with paddles, and learning the balance. Two did something wrong and spun upside down in the seawater.

37

"Help him right his boat!" I growled. Six and Four flipped his craft and Two came up sputtering water and soaking wet, but alive. Ten said, "You look like a drowned rat!"

"Dead rat—I like it!" added Two in a deadpan manner. Wolf-grins fell like rain in a storm. The next time someone said "dead rat" everyone looked at Two, but he just shook his head and ignored it.

We all took the kayaks a little more seriously from then on, testing our balance, practicing dipping in the oars and gliding around. Forty-five minutes later, after stowing the gear around our legs and sealing it against the damp, the pack was ready to go.

So we did.

Behind the breakwater the water was smooth as glass, and once we got to the open waters of the Puget Sound, the water was behaving itself. Our Kayaks slid up and down the waves with ease. Things were starting out well. We were on course to tiptoe around the southern tip of Bainbridge Island, then head north up its west side, and hit Poulsbo before dawn. Then we would cross the Hood Canal, making our way through the mountains and on to the Hoh Rain Forest on the western side of the Olympic National Forest. The Hoh Rain Forest YouTube channel had been mesmerizing, and the area met our needs with plenty of room to grow. It said that there had once been wolves roaming these lands, but man killed them all. We were going to restore balance to the former paradise. It would be a promised land for Wolves, a land waiting to be built and an ecology to be restored. And we are a lot harder to kill than our ancestors.

We'd come so far in such a relatively short time, from caged Dogs to proud Wolves, from creatures who didn't stand upright, to walking among the humans without arousing suspicion. From the first burnt meat show watched eagerly from the bushes to our mastery of Google as a search engine and YouTube as a teacher of skills.

We devoured everything this human world around us had to offer and realized that we would rather build a home far from humanity, in the endless rainforest, close enough to smell the salt of the Pacific Ocean.

Something about being out here in the salt, far from land, made my mind wander to things I didn't understand. I was remembering those sparkly vampires that were said to live in nearby Forks. We had watched a couple of confusing documentaries about those creatures. Not that I was worried; we were Wolves, forest creatures. And the vampires seemed to be more concerned with themselves and pretty girls and didn't care much for forests. There were those beasts that claimed to be wolves, but they appeared not to be skilled fighters. How did they do that changing thing? I wondered…

A salt spray from a paddle splashing me in the face brought my attention back to the present. Leaning into my paddle, I dug deeper into the water, forcing the group to pick up the pace.

Sometimes it's good to be alpha.

CHAPTER 7

Islay Scotch & Dancing Bears

Commander Elwha lifted his Dog control unit and examined it in the spotlight over his cherrywood desk. It was still shiny. He put it back in his belt sheath next to his sidearm. They had arrived too late to capture his runaway Dogs, who had apparently been holed up on the island just next door! He didn't understand why they hadn't been spotted, or inadvertently betrayed themselves much sooner.

The Commander oversaw the training of the engineered biological guard units called Dogs. He had to have a firm hand; the monsters had more Wolf genes than human and could be difficult to manage. He still had two remaining packs of the dangerous creatures, though. Both were being good Dogs, but his missing hounds worried him like a toothache he couldn't heal. They were doing things they'd never been conditioned to do! And he had seen for himself the gate vid where Dog Three had walked upright to the keypad and punched in the numbers to open the gate as if he'd been opening it for years. Exactly how long had Dog Three been able to do that?

Far stranger was the rest of the pack's awkward, upright strut that followed. They were even wearing clothing, if you could call the mishmash of garish fashion and fur clothes. Suddenly he remembered his aged Siberian grandfather telling him about dancing bears.

"It's not how graceful a bear dances, but that it dances at all! This is simply not in a bear's nature and is the result of long, hard training," Grandpa had told him. Dancing bears, walking dogs... there must be a reason this old story had popped up in his mind!

The Dogs must be imitating things they saw, or things someone had trained into them. There was no way they could have become able to think critically, strategize, and take action in the short time they'd been out of his control. Who was messing with his runaway Dogs?

The Commander scowled and turned to his com display. His men had lost them in the forest, and it was sheer luck that a perimeter guard had seen them as they leapt down from the forest's edge to the small beach. They quickly lost them in the storm, and for a moment he had wanted to use one of the other packs to trail the escapees.

Then he remembered that exposing good Dogs to bad-Dog behavior never leads anywhere desirable. He didn't want the other Dogs getting any ideas; that's why he had isolated his bio-guard units from each other in the first place. This kept social diseases such as "resistance-to-authority" or "running-away" from spreading to contaminate the other Dogs. Bio-lab 101, for bloody hell's sake.

The Commander's sailors had picked up the trail again in Port Townsend, where his bad Dogs had boarded a ferry! How the hell did they figure out how to buy ferry tickets? Where did they learn about, and lay their paws on, money? His head was starting to hurt, so he popped a couple of Naproxen Sodium with three fingers of an eighteen-year-old Islay Scotch.

41

That helped a little bit.

CHAPTER 8

Götterdämmerung

We slid quietly into the Poulsbo marina in our kayaks, quickly finding sheltered spots to hide the feisty little boats. We had grown quite fond of them by now. My pack walked uphill from the busy waterside taverns and restaurants, through a pitiful park with only a handful of trees, and up to a brick structure on a hill. It was huge. Seven said it was called Safeway and, in exchange for money, we could get anything we needed there. It also had free Wi-Fi, which seemed to be important. Once inside, I found myself captivated by the Wing bar. It smelled heavenly.

"How much money do we have left from that pack of humans?" I asked Thirteen.

"Enough," she replied with a silent Wolf chuckle.

Seven, Eleven, and Four clustered around their tablets in the seating area of Safeway by a fireplace that burned without using up the logs. The colorful occupants of several seats were odd enough that three partially shaved Wolves fit right in. Our tech trio got straight to work. They eventually found a bus tour of the Hoh Rain Forest. It was a four-day round trip, with a stop each night in a picturesque forest hotel.

Thirteen, our money Wolf, was able to get a something called a group rate for all of us, using one of the credit cards we'd harvested near Pioneer Square in old Seattle. The tour bus left Poulsbo at ten the next morning.

That was the plan; by the next night we would be there. In the Hoh Rain Forest. Our new home!

After finishing up and shutting down our tablets, Thirteen made sure to leave the credit card behind on the table to muddy our financial trail. Walking away from the humans, we joined the rest of the pack under the blackberry grove on the west side of the parking garage. I had bought out the buffalo-chicken wing bar, so I was greeted with lots of sniffing and tail wagging.

We fell asleep beneath the arching ceiling of a huge blackberry thicket. In the morning we returned to Safeway to shave our faces and forearms again in the grocery store's restrooms before resuming our journey, walking the road in dawn's early light.

We walked in groups of three or four to avoid suspicion. While a couple of towering hipsters with beards and backpacks aren't exactly unheard of in these parts, we did kind of stand out.

I couldn't wait to get to the promised land and to start building a life for us, for our pack. I wanted to be completely free of the Commander, and humans in general. I wanted to carve out territory where a Wolf didn't have to hide what he was.

I was getting pretty tired of shaving my head, too.

Five stopped and went alert. Everyone focused on my second, who stood frozen, listening. I couldn't hear anything! Then I realized that it was silent. The human world is generally a noisy place if you have good hearing. All the normal city noises we'd grown used to continued. It was the background that was missing. The insect world, the dogs on leashes, the screaming gulls and foul-mouthed crows—all dead silent, as if holding their breath. I felt a chill run down my spine. Then somewhere way off, a dog was going crazy, howling as if the world was ending.

That was when the first tremor hit, knocking everybody off their paws. The sidewalk beneath our us snapped into chunks, while we were bouncing in the quake violence, unable to regain our feet. The noise was terrible, even after the first tremor finally ended. My ears felt shredded. I got up angry for a moment—until I turned to see what Five and some of the others were staring at.

All the buildings and land between our hilltop and the marina had collapsed. A filthy wall of mud, saltwater and broken trees was rushing our way, sweeping everything before it. It was thirty meters of towering wave and growing.

"Run for the Safeway roof!" I ordered. Then the next tremor hit.

This one blew up the sun.

At least that's what it felt like, just like when the Commander pushed the bad-Dog button, delivering an electroshock explosion to my nervous system that left me in convulsions of tongue-biting white light. I felt lost and helpless to escape the terrible pain as I bounced and broke helplessly on the jagged pavement fragments.

But we are Wolves.

The clarity of fury took over and I fell into battle-mode.

The world around me slow to a glacial pace as what I had once forgotten returns. I phase into base reality. I am in Flux.

The ability and desire to use language falls from me in a burst of brilliant white light that doesn't hurt my eyes. Staring around in slow motion, I drink in the world around me in untranslated bites of newness that I process in bursts

45

of understanding. All the synapses in my brain surrender to the visceral intellect at the base of my skull.

I exult in it!

The jagged boulders of cement, asphalt, and iron seem to melt under me in slow motion, and I sense I have all the time in the world. I push my center of gravity forward and gently roll to my feet. I step onto a meter-wide piece of pavement with my right paw as it slowly rotates past. It lifts me to the next glacial step through the frozen landscape, silent and monochrome, as I carefully chose my path through the earthquake's wave of tumbling destruction.

My pack has joined me in base reality and follows my lead through the molasses flood of smashed debris and ragged fragments of concrete. I point uphill. We run, accelerated in juiced up speed across the slowly shaking earth, leaping from stone to stone.

It's not as hard as it looks.

Not for a Wolf in Flux.

At the rooftop, we shifted out of battle-mode, scanning the ruined land around us from the safety of the red brick monolith's roof. The muddy torrent is relentlessly surging through Poulsbo, wiping the earth clean of man's work wherever it touches. The neighborhood uphill from this grocery store is on fire, and the fire department has been washed away in a flashing light display, leaving only the oily seawater and floating garbage in its wake. The waves continue to eat everything in sight, but the thousands of plastic pieces of flotsam are unsinkable. The waves start slapping the roof where we stand, the raucous tsunami's hunger unsatisfied.

Time to move.

CHAPTER 9

"Who Set the World on Fire?"

We climbed down the backside of the building and dropped into neck deep water. We quickly moved uphill. The fires were beginning to run wild already—there was no longer any force remaining to fight them and the flames were gorging themselves. The entire neighborhood above us was going up in an inferno of towering flames, transforming the trees surrounding the houses into a loud blaze that devoured whatever it touched in scorching fury.

From the look of the two remaining roads, our tour bus wasn't going to be arriving anytime soon. That was okay, we were getting used to walking like humans.

I pointed north.

"That way," I said. My pack formed up around me, closer than usual; that was to be expected in these treacherous terrains. Out of the water and into the fire.

"Go to all fours when you need to," I said, but no one did. "Expect aftershocks. Beware any falling buildings, don't get too close. You are not allowed to get smashed by falling debris!" I ordered.

Lots of silent laughter, Wolf style.

The heat from the blazing houses and pine trees crowding the street was a blowtorch nose-smack when you got too close. We were just able to tolerate trotting down the center of the road in single file; the ambient heat was starting to make the asphalt a little sticky. By the time we were halfway through the neighborhood, the stink of singed Wolf hair was everywhere, in spite of our shaved heads and arms. We ignored it but were relieved when the heat finally lessened somewhat as the houses we passed were more spread out.

I came to a stop.

Standing in the middle of the fire-lit street was a little human girl. She was staring at the place where she used to live. Must be the place where her family had just been burned up, I realized. Her black hair was long and tangled, and the ends of her locks and eyebrows looked singed. A fire-damaged dolly was safely tucked under her left armpit. The little girl registered our arrival with a glance our direction, but it didn't seem to matter. She just kept staring hollow-eyed into the fire where her home used to be.

I didn't know what to do.

I know I had pups when I was human, but I don't really remember much about them. So, I just stood silently beside her for a few minutes as she gazed into the blaze that had taken everything from her. I stared into the fire too, trying to see what she saw, while at the same time certain that I didn't really want to see it. After a while her hand reached up, grasping and squeezing my paw. I squeezed back, and she seemed to take comfort from this.

We stood there watching the raging fire for an unmeasured period, and then she turned to face me. She reached out and climbed up into my arms. After a moment I nodded to my pack, and we resumed our journey. If the limpness of her body, and the regularity of her breath were any clue, the little girl was already sleeping soundly. That was very good, because we saw things that night no pup should have to see.

It never occurred to us to leave her to her fate. We are pack and cherish cubs. Keeping her safe with us felt right, just like *pack* felt right. Maybe she didn't have to be a Wolf to be part of our pack. Or maybe, just being in our pack would make her a Wolf?

Questions for another day.

Terrible times can have beauty, and treasure is sometimes found in the most tragic of places.

Sunrise approached, full of scarlet and orange from the forest fires chewing their way across the Hood canal shoreline. The smoke from the fires and masonry dust hung in the air like some warped gray blanket. By now we had begun to pant from all the ash and dust, so I had us all wrap our faces in damp clothing, crude but effective breathing masks.

We needed to go to ground soon. It wasn't safe for my Wolves to be seen in the light of day. I was sure Commander Elwha—if he were still alive—hadn't given up on us either, even with the devastation of the quake. We knew he was never going to give up until he found us.

I had my pack spread out, searching for a refuge from the day. Nine found several baseball diamonds outlined by burning trees beside the highway on our right and three multistory buildings, noisily popping and cracking with fire.

Exploring, we found several short, earth-sheltered dugout buildings on the edge of the baseball diamonds. From there we moved into the abandoned dressing rooms behind the dugouts. It was actually cool in there. The air was clear, too, and didn't make us cough when we took off our improvised masks.

We quickly downed our protein shakes and fell asleep in a mound of Wolves, with the human cub tucked in neatly in the center. Everyone was exhausted and dove into sleep like broke pearl divers.

There are worse ways to end a bad day than in a warm pile of Wolves.

CHAPTER 10

Commander Elwha's New World

The Commander was knee deep in paperwork at his Remote Command Center, down in the secret labs beneath Indian Island Naval Magazine, when the world as he knew it came to an end.

His Remote Command was situated on the main level of the sequestered laboratories, and from there he could run a war or an empire, should need be. The hardened, watertight installation was designed to survive a direct nuclear strike to the base. Not easily accessed, it required a fifteen-minute commute from the front door down to the labs. It was a small world in and of itself, containing executive kitchens, offices, almost comfortable bunks, gyms, entertainment centers, state of the art research labs, and even a small store.

This was the place where the first Dogs were created from suicidal volunteer Marines.

Someone of high rank had decided that the problem of high military suicide rates might as well be put to good use, so they began offering signing bonuses for a one-way trip to forget-everything-land. The despondent warriors could have their oblivion, and the Navy got their mind-wiped bodies to play genetic rewrite games with.

His most successful creations were the Dogs, who had ended up with more timber wolf genes than human, deadly fighters with a pack mentality. They required a very firm hand. The Commander enjoyed that part.

The applying discipline part.

The downside was all the paperwork. He couldn't have gotten the level of commander without being skilled in administrative documentation and knowledgeable in military protocol and procedures. At least he had well-trained adjuncts and secretaries to help carry the load. The scotch helped, too.

It was an unremarkable afternoon, just like any other, until sailors started bouncing off the ceilings.

Everything that could fall to the ground did, only to be bounced back into the air by the heaving floor. The earthquake continued unabated, showing no sign of giving up its violent ways. Soon bones began breaking as they kept hitting an angry floor. The Commander knew this, because he could feel his left elbow and right ankle fracture. Everyone was getting seriously beat-up by the quake and the tumbling furniture. Then the entryway to the secret base cracked open like an egg and muddy water began fountaining up from a fissure in the floor. Someone hit the *seal* button, and the watertight portals spun closed, but not before the Commander saw ragged bodies floating in the rising water. The water had a scarlet hue.

After what seemed like an eternity, the ground stopped quaking, and everything grew still. He found himself on his back on the floor, shoved up against a battered file cabinet that lay on its side. Someone was noisily vomiting nearby; the Commander's stomach thought that sounded like a good idea and violently ejected his lunch. He wiped his mouth clean with a white handkerchief as got to his feet. Glaring around him, he sought a target for his displeasure, then shook his head. There would be time for anger later.

"Officer! What happened? How many injured? Techs, seal everything and go to internal air supply. Coms! Henderson, get me the Pentagon! Lee, base integrity! Everyone knows their job—just follow protocols and man your station if you can. If not report to…" Commander Elwha glanced at the medical officer working on someone missing a leg.

Without looking up the medical officer sang out "Triage in Lab E".

"Lab E," the Commander repeated loudly. In a quieter voice he asked, "What the hell happened? Did someone drop a nuke on us?" He then hopped to his control center with as much dignity as possible. There wasn't much of the desk left… or his dignity.

A Medic appeared at his side and steered the Commander into a hastily righted chair. The Commander ignored the poking and bandaging, using his good arm to shove the debris off his desk and clear his command screen. It was dead. The medic yanked on his arm. He glared at the medic, then turned to face the open area of the foyer, dining room, gym, security, and environmental controls. Everyone was doing exactly what they had been trained to do under the circumstances.

A few minutes later, a semblance of order had been restored to the underground complex and the injured were being tended. Knots of marines were tracing connections, attempting to restore communications to the outside world. Another team was working to open an auxiliary exit tunnel, in order to go topside to survey the damage. Unfortunately, the lock's mechanisms had been warped out of shape by the earthquake, When they did get it partially open, cold saltwater began spewing from the escape tunnel. The marines hastily sealed it again. There shouldn't have been any water in that tunnel, even though they were forty meters below sea level.

The Commander was not pleased.

"Radiation levels don't indicate nuclear weapons," a research scientist offered, "And the number of conventional explosions required to produce this kind of seismic disturbance for such an extended period are statistically unachievable. I don't think that's what happened." The Commander turned to glare at him, urging the scientist to continue. If the scientist had been tuned into nonverbal communication, he wouldn't have opened his mouth in the first place, so he didn't pick up on the Commander's expectation either. A research assistant named Greg kicked him in the shin and nodded to the commanding officer.

"Oh, I… um… suspect it was an earthquake of massive proportions. One possibility is that the Juan de Fuca plate has slid under the North American plate in the Cascadia Subduction Zone. In any case, the movement from the quake is wreaking havoc on the GPS systems and magnetic compasses. That's why we are having trouble reaching topside. Ahh… we may not have seen the worst of it yet. If the scientists who predicted this quake are right, a big tidal wave is likely to have hit us in the last five minutes," the clueless scientist finished, rubbing his shin and shooting eye-daggers at his assistant.

"Great! Tidal waves too. I should have just stayed in bed this morning," the Commander grumbled as he tried once again to coax his screens to life.

Two hours later his screens scrabbled to life and Indian Island rejoined the world of Navy communications. What they found wasn't pretty.

"Our own Special Weapons vaults remain secure, if difficult to access. There's a lot of secondary damage to the structures that didn't collapse. A massive tectonic event has occurred, and the landscape around us is virtually unrecognizable. Damage appears to cover the entire western seaboard. It's a mess up here, Commander," the Com officer at Kitsap-Bangor admitted.

The Commander rocked backward in his chair. So, it was true. The nation's enemies would be quick to take advantage of America's catastrophe. Especially the damned Maoists. He leaned forward and began barking orders.

The Naval Magazine on Indian Island stored ammunition and weapons for the Navy. This ranged from sidearms to smart hydrogen bombs, from guided missiles to stores of gel explosives. Munitions were spread out in underground structures designed to contain any accidental explosions to one unit. If all precautions failed at once, the whole base could go up, leaving nothing behind but floating ash and a huge underwater hole where an island used to be.

"Henderson! Where the hell is my Pentagon line? This is a priority situation and we need to get some support coming our way now!" The Commander focused his gaze on his command screen—there were lights going off all over the place! Looked like all transpacific communications were down. All the fiber-optic conduits east and south of the Olympic Peninsula were severed as well. Satellite was wonky but still working. Well, would be working if his big antenna dish with its wandering ways hadn't taken off for the nearest deep ravine.

Seven hours later, after everybody had been working non-stop, full command channels were re-established. The Commander had spent the time trying to get someone with pull at the Pentagon. Everyone was too busy to listen to his demands of resources and evacuation of his injured by Seahawks out of Kitsap-Bangor Navy Base.

He was trying to take care of his people and found himself ignored instead.

LA, San Francisco, Portland, and Seattle were all reporting hundreds of thousands dead and there were millions of people missing. They were getting all the attention and resources of a shaken nation.

Having the president tweet "indigenous missing on the Olympic Peninsula are a waste of national resources in a time of emergency. They don't pay any taxes like the rest of us, so they move to the back of the line," was the last straw. The Commander's father's tribe had been paddling these waters long before the white man showed up. And he paid plenty of taxes.

Lying white supremist! he thought.

That was the turning point.

That was the exact moment the Commander said, "To hell with you, Mr. President!" It was the moment he decided to go for the gold. To found his own country, run *his* way. For life. He would not be unlike a god, if you squinted just right!

This was not as unlikely a possibility as it sounded.

First of all, Commander Elwha was now the ranking officer on the Olympic Peninsula, so, he immediately seized control of all Naval forces west of Seattle and north of Tacoma. Bremerton, Silverdale, Port Angeles, Sequim, and Port Townsend all reported in, with initial casualty rates exceeding sixty-five percent on the bases. Significant ammunition dumps and naval magazines had been lost.

The Commander slammed his desk with his good arm. They had said the big quake wouldn't ever be this bad! The damned experts had insisted that the worst-case scenario would be less than twenty percent casualties! That was considered an acceptable number by the good old boys at the Pentagon.

The Commander dispatched two teams to assist in rescue and recovery in nearby Port Townsend and Sequim.

Farther westward would have to wait. In the meantime, he directed all local resources to focus on the Bremerton shipyard. His priority was getting the Tridents and fighting ships out of Kitsap-Bangor Naval base and into what remained of the Strait of Juan de Fuca.

The enemy was sure to take advantage of their moment of vulnerability, and his forces were the only thing between an invasion fleet and the homeland. Commander Elwha intended to give them more than they bargained for, even if no one else could see the threat like he did.

The Commander also knew that resources were going to become scarce very quickly, and he had no inclination to compromise his own safety by stripping his base bare to supply someone else. He currently had over a thousand mouths left to feed, so he rolled up his sleeves and got to work.

"Do you think the Commander will let us investigate the fault line?" the clueless scientist asked his research assistant Greg. Greg just stared back at him for a long pause.

"What?" demanded the scientist.

"The Commander is a megalomaniac disrespected Native American with nuclear weapons. And you want to jiggle his elbow and ask for a field trip?" Greg asked.

CHAPTER 11

Payback Plans

Once he had local assessment and recovery running efficiently, the Commander turned his attention to the thirty-six bio-pods clustered in groups of nine in the covert laboratory, concealed in a high-security enclave at the end of the long corridor behind him. He turned to face it.

Each pod held a volunteer sailor's body undergoing genetic reprogramming and splicing with proprietary wolf DNA. In another month, the Commander would have a new pack of Dogs to train. This would bring his base back up to strength after losing an entire pack when Dog Three went bad.

He gritted his teeth at the thought, but then made himself relax, at least on the outside, and grumbled, "Screw that!" again and started cursing Dog Three. There was going to be hell to pay when he finally dragged that mangy mutt back home. He mumbled semi-audible threats all the way up the underground complex emergency escape ladder. When he got to the top, he immediately wanted to turn back.

The fires were eighty-nine percent controlled, thanks to the determined crews who had trained for this. The defensive line of the inner base was now fortified and mined. Grim sailors and marines manned all of the base's entry points, waiting to give some pay-back to the enemy, whoever it was. Fighting men are trained to fight back. They weren't that particular about who they blasted into the next world, either.

Somebody was going to have to pay.

CHAPTER 12

After the Apocalypse

Sirens shrieked incessantly as the sun rose, not quieting until late morning. Not long after that, the sounds of gunfire and the ugly sounds humans make as they die began to dominate. We were safe and cozy in our hidden refuge and remained so until the sun started to go down and we got up. Licuado protein shakes for everybody, including the cub. Then we geared up while Five and Twelve checked things out in the falling night. When we got the all-clear, the human cub climbed up on my back into a harness Nine had contrived and we walked into the night.

The narrow gap of land between the highway and the Hood Canal had become a smoldering charcoal factory. Most of the houses were burned to the ground. Red embers piled everywhere, so we had to watch where we stepped. There were human and dog bodies all over the place, too, smelling like burnt meat. I really didn't want to notice how good that smelled. It had been a while since we'd had the chance to eat meat. Didn't see any sign of cats though; those spooky bastards never stick around when there's trouble.

The cub had her arms and legs wrapped around my wide back tighter than was necessary, and I could feel the small human's hot breath in my ear as she watched everything over my left shoulder. She was quiet at first.

After an hour or so, she whispered, "You're kind of furry," in my ear. But of course, we Wolves have very good hearing, so the entire pack heard her.

"That's because I'm a Wolf," I responded. Cubs question everything to learn about the world. I answered as best I could.

"Oh," she said warmly. "I've heard of wolves! Didn't they eat Little Red Riding Hood?"

"Well, my pack didn't—we don't eat humans unless they're our enemies. Enemies are dangerous, and we need to keep them from hurting others," I explained. "We tell the truth to our pups, so they grow up wise. That the way we'll do things in our pack."

"Oh. I wish you'd eat the bad man that grabbed Mommy. He was very bad," she said fervently.

I thought of what the bad guys in old Seattle had wanted to do and growled. I didn't mean to, it just slipped out. But she wasn't scared at all.

"Yeah, me too," she said sadly. "Are you some kind of dog-man?" she whispered in my ear. I stifled the kind of growl that quickly goes sub-woofer.

Then I sighed.

"Once we were slaves and ate gruel from rusty troughs like animals. The sailors called us Dogs, but then I figured out that we were Wolves. Wolves don't live that way. So that is why we ran away," I said. "Now we are not running *away* anymore, we are running *to* something. We're heading to the Hoh Rain Forest. That's where we are going to build a village in the forest, a place where we can live free as Wolves are

61

meant to. We are pack and family. Now you are pack, too." I paused to get my words right. She went very still.

"Now you are my cub, my family, and part of my pack. You will never have to be alone again," I explained.

The cub didn't reply, but just held on tighter. I felt warm drops that smelled of salt on my neck for the next kilometer, but I didn't mind. This one had lost everything. Now she had a place in the world.

All cubs need a pack.

CHAPTER 13

On the Road

We walked Highway Three North carefully, pseudo-hipsters with too much hair and too many guns, our noses, ears, and eyes saw everything clearly. We were becoming accustomed to passing for humans, but we knew we were simply Wolves in long coats.

My pack was arranged around me in a tight configuration well-suited to threading our way through a graveyard of dead grendels and sometimes live, human ones. The dead metal monsters creeped me out the most. Even if YouTube made them seem harmless, I still felt distrust on an epic scale.

We passed looters and worse with regularity. I was surprised at how quickly the humans reverted to their deadly ways once the fear of punishment was no longer hanging over their heads. It had been less than twenty-four hours since the massive quake hit. It was as if they'd just given up on law and the government and started grabbing what they could for themselves.

Or maybe the apocalypse just brings out the mean in some folks.

A blond human almost as tall as I am, with dark smudges of ash across his face, planted himself in my path. His fifteen bullyboys were equally grimy. They all stepped into the section of highway we were about to enter, cutting us off. I focused on him with an intensity that was almost intimate. He stared back, a wicked smile tossed in.

The blond boss was strapped up with an auto-shotgun and a forty-five semi-automatic with an extended magazine. His pack had a plenitude of armament, but he had distributed his resources poorly. Two of his men, whose primary weapons appeared to be close quarter sub-machine guns, were placed too far away to be effective. A guy with machetes was sandwiched between two guys with modern assault weapons. One of his riflemen was also poorly placed. This pack's alpha appeared to be new to the business of slaughter, and from what I saw, probably wasn't going to live long enough to reproduce. Just as well.

"He's the bad man... the man who got mommy. Eat him, Wolf!" the cub demanded earnestly in my ear. I snorted and proudly thought, *Spoken like a Wolf.*

"Quiet walking, eyes closed like we talked about," I said gently, and my cub squeezed her eye tightly shut. Then I focused on the guy with the blades.

He noticed.

The machete-guy leered back at me with a practiced sneer that told me this wasn't his first time cutting a way to his objective, one body at a time. I glanced back at the blond boss. He demanded that we hand over all our weapons, money, and females immediately. He thought he was in charge.

He was wrong.

I looked him directly in the eyes, alpha to alpha.

He flinched, and it was on.

"One, Seven, and Eleven, Uzis. Two, Thirteen and Six, pin the leader, remove bodyguards. Four, Five, and Ten, on me… Machete. Eight, Nine, and Twelve, rifles. Go!" I ordered snarling my words so the humans wouldn't distinguish the meaning.

I phased into Flux… as if I have all the time in the world, *because I do*, in the space between heartbeats. I intuitively know that I need to take out the machete-guy first, then the blond leader. Weapons and females, my ass; we are pack!

I slide my Bowie knife from its sheath and briefly come to guard position, as I drink in the rich tapestry of smell and sound around me. They paint the world in nuances of scent, and I hear everything around me in detailed tones. Sound and smell alone are powerful enough for Wolves to surpass a puny human's eyesight and anemic hearing. My eyes aren't bad either.

I strike at Machete-guy's right knee with my knife, and his blade replies, coming close enough to part the hair on the back of my hand without breaking skin, before I pull away. He is very fast, and his blades are razor sharp. Luckily, I am faster, and my Bowie is sharper still.

What really is going to hurt him is that I operate in Flux. He's slowed down by the pace of his logic, while I am free to cut through the chaff and strike intuitively. He's the butter, and I am the hot knife.

When the moment reaches fullness, I slip forward under his strike to draw my Bowie across his throat and the right carotid artery. I step past to avoid most of the crimson spray, and freshly sheered copper floods my nose. I carefully examine my work as I slide by him; I have cut his head half off. It lolls to the right. I feel neither triumph nor pain.

65

In Flux, I have no fear, or compassion, no guilt or shame which speeds my response considerably. I instinctively know what to do, faster without emotions.

I keep moving forward. I sense his torso collapsing at the knees behind me, then falling to the floor in a graceless jumble.

I don't look back.

I lunge into two new enemies in my path at the same time, moving like lightning, and everything else is crawling. They fall apart and suddenly I am two meters away from the blond alpha. He is trying to bring his shotgun to bear on me, his face distorted by the effort.

He is too slow.

I have no problem dodging his first shotgun blast, but he doesn't lose focus. He's stubborn, and keeps shooting at me, doing his best to blow off one or two of my body parts. He never seems to get it right.

I am within reach now, so I do. I tear away the shotgun, bend his right hand the wrong way and rotate. He screams in pain, then screams again as he watches his remaining pack vanish under the devout attention of Wolves. He looks back at me.

Now he understands.

I rip his right arm off, discard it, and go for the jugular. I bite his head clean off and step out of the way as it rolls off the highway. They're heavier than you would expect. Heads.

I can feel the hot breath of our cub on my neck, rapid and shallow. I re-enter mundane reality quickly, as if someone has splashed me with cold water.

"Cub, you can open your eyes now. Are you hurt?" I asked, moving carefully away from the highway and into a stand of unburnt trees away from the scene of slaughter. I didn't want Rachel to have to see that. I lifted her off my back to examine her for wounds. There were none. Seven and

Twelve were immediately at my side, sniffing her deeply, making sure the pack's only pup was undamaged. She giggled, "That tickles," but enjoyed the physical reassurance of Wolves. After a little while I picked up the small human and settled her back in her harness. We moved out, sticking to the burned forest instead of using the broken roadway.

"I'm okay! But that was really scary, even with my eyes closed tight," she whispered, hoarsely. After a moment, she added, "But I was kind of glad you ate him, too. I hate bad men."

"We didn't really eat him, pup. That's just how we think of it when we have to put down an enemy. That we ate him and chewed the bones like our ancestors. But we are more than they were, so we don't do that anymore. But yes cub, I think I hate bad humans, too," I said. "My name is Three. Will you tell me yours?" I asked carefully. Humans are kind of sensitive sometimes; lots of vid-clips said that. She didn't respond immediately.

"I'm Rachel Adamson," she admitted after a moment. "What kinda name is Three?" she asked.

"What kind of name is *Adam's son*? Don't look like a son to me," I responded, maybe a little defensively. Could be I'm a little touchy about some things, having re-started life as a caged Dog. Then I sighed.

"In the beginning I was known as 'Dog Three', but that was a lie; I am a Wolf who used to be a human, a fighting sailor. So now I'm just Three. And I am the alpha of this pack. Unfortunately, I can't remember very much of when I used to be human," I admitted.

"I think Three is a nice name," Rachel declared kindly. "This is Toni," she said, sticking her singed doll in my face.

I tried to think of what people on YouTube would do. Couldn't come up with anything, so I just sort of patted the

67

dolly on the head and changed the subject. Rachel noticed but decided to let it pass and not say anything.

The grace of little girls should never be underestimated.

CHAPTER 14

Just Not Yet

I sent Five and a team to loot our attacker's corpses. The trees were still burning, the smoke was thick in places. This created a surreal landscape of sullen orange coals and curtains of gray smoke that only broke when we reached the water's edge, a ways south of the Hood Canal Bridge. Five's team rejoined us. The pack continued paralleling the road for roughly two kilometers before we ran out of room, squeezed between a highway jammed with four-wheel grendels and the water.

Lit up bright as day, the entrance to the bridge had been hardened into a huge temporary defensive structure mostly comprised of armored concrete pilons, each a meter high and four meters long. Marine gunners crouched behind huge anti-aircraft guns and smart-tech missile launchers. A flock of vulture-drones roosted on the upper part of the six-meter-high structure. That was a lot of firepower pointed our way.

I wrinkled my nose in distaste but had to admit it was a formidable barrier to our planned route. There must have been close to seventy marines swarming on this end of the bridge. There didn't appear to be a middle part of the bridge anymore. The surviving section near us hung out over the water for at least one-hundred meters. We could see even bigger guns out there, poking up over more of the armored pilons.

We retreated, falling back into the shelter of a burned-out rental equipment yard. There, we crouched in shadow, building a picture from what each Wolf had observed. We each tended to notice different parts of the picture. Twelve was all about means of surreptitious entry. Seven studied the antenna and small dishes that connected the different outposts. Five noted the glinting of eyes he could make out behind the guns and sniper nests, but lost count as they moved around. I turned to face the water.

We watched quietly as the war ships limped by, brightly lit up and swarming with angry sailors manning deck guns. The Trident submarines were each escorted by workboats, but all we saw was a vast fish shape swimming between funny little boats. Only one was above water, and it resembled a giant grendel shark too damaged to submerge. It was scary. The ships and boats were fleeing Kitsap-Bangor Naval Base and seemed quite willing to destroy anything or anyone that got in their way. Other smaller fighting ships patrolled both sides of the passage, with a man standing behind a really big gun out front. I could almost taste the weapon's name but didn't bother to retrieve it.

The Hood Canal was uncrossable at this point.

"Eight, Thirteen, and Two, scout underneath the bridge area. Five, the canal edge through here. What happened here? Why are all the broken ships lighting up the channel like New Year's Eve on YouTube? Where are they going? Are they running away or toward something…?" I stopped there. Four questions were enough. Couldn't hear the answer if my mouth was running.

I nodded to Five. He held my eye a fraction longer than usual, then leapt to do my bidding. Being second in rank wasn't enough for some Wolves, which is why I was keeping an eye on him.

"Seven, what's our next best route to the rainforest and how many days to get there?" I asked, as we waited and re-hydrated. She pulled out the new satellite phone Twelve had found for her and began figuring it out with Eleven. Nerds and their phones.

I put Rachel down and sat against the rental center's side wall facing the lot. All these metal grendels crouching in the yard around us were making me a little uneasy. Rachel climbed up into my lap and started playing with her Toni doll. I rested, mentally sorting our options.

Then I realized that our cub was talking to the doll, telling her to listen when the alpha said to shut their eyes 'cause they had to get rid of bad men. Toni was too young. Then she told the doll that someday she was going to open her eyes like a real Wolf. Just not yet.

I hugged her gently. She me hugged back. She was going to be an exceptional Wolf someday.

Just not yet.

CHAPTER 15

Coup d'état

The Commander peered wearily into his screens. The limping exodus from the shipyards and Kitsap-Bangor Naval Base was taking too long! But his new navy was slowly assembling in the Strait of Juan de Fuca, at least what was left of it.

There had been a few who refused to acknowledge his authority. The Commander knew he had to be ruthless in his initial execution of power, and he easily rose to the situation. His specialist team's stealth drones carried noise-suppressed offensive weaponry, firing .776 caliber explosive rounds. He had always enjoyed applying discipline.

It was needed now, so he dealt it out.

By twenty-three hundred, none remained to oppose him. His new nation was born in blood and quake, and he was going to build it into a major international power, respected, or at least feared, by all.

He also planned on being emperor for life, but it was expedient to remain "the Commander" for a spell. One had to orchestrate everything, and there was always a pace to these things. Tyrants aren't born overnight.

The Indian Island Naval Magazine had been restored to working form over the last twenty-six hours. The lights and electronic defenses were now operational, and the underground barracks were just coming back online, ready for an exhausted navy to lay down their heads and catch a few winks.

Of course, that's when everything went directly to hell again.

"Priority alert! The People's Republic of China aircraft carrier Qinghai, accompanied by a fleet of destroyers, is inbound; course currently set for Vancouver, B.C. All forces Red Alert! Enemy contact in six hours. Red Alert..." Marc Christiansen, the only remaining base commander of Bangor, growled into the priority comm channel. As the last of the special forces left to defend the once proud Base Bangor, he was way understrength. He didn't care—he had no intention of abandoning his post. Wasn't the Navy way, wasn't his way. They were SEALs. No foreign navy was going to take possession of the ravaged naval base.

"Acknowledged, Bangor. Do not go gently into that dark night, boys. Indian Island, Out," Commander Elwha said. Then a new message came over the international channel.

"Attention, British Columbia. The Peoples Republic of China has come to assist you in these difficult times. We are here at the request of many Chinese citizens. Our mission is to protect the one-point-four million ethnic Chinese affected by this environmental disaster. Do not interfere with our humanitarian actions. We are fully prepared to answer aggression in kind," the Qinghai broadcast. The broadcast began to repeat. The Commander leaned back in his chair and put his hands over his burning eyes. After a few seconds, he leapt to his feet.

"Great! Now the damn Chinese are invading! We need to *get there the fastest with the mostest* before she offloads troops on the mainland!" the Commander shouted. All tired sailors knew that, in times of war, you just had to push yourself and keep going.

Nobody slept that night.

CHAPTER 16

Tyger, Tyger, Burning Bright

"Prepare to launch," she rumbled to her team.

Major Malgato leaned farther forward in the front of the landing craft, her weight bringing down the bow of the craft to present a lower silhouette. "Launch!" ordered the major, and they were abruptly dropped from the stern of a frigate into moderate seas. "Engage!" she ordered the engineer, once they fully resurfaced and everyone could breathe again.

Tonight's moon was mostly hidden by clouds, but occasionally a brilliant beam of silver pierced the clouds to spotlight the oily black sea. Malgato suddenly found her striped face bathed in pewter and flashed her teeth, as only a Tiger can, gleaming ivory in the moon's cold light. Then it was dark again. Twenty minutes later, the craft ran up on a pebble beach in noisy triumph and came to a stop.

Tigers poured out in liquid grace and took up position. Only then did Malgato step onto the sand of the Dungeness spit, in the former region of the United States known as the Olympic Peninsula, and smile.

It was by no means a pretty smile.

These elite Tigers were former People's Republic special forces *volunteers* who had been mind-wiped and re-engineered with a multitude of Siberian tiger genes. Once the Tigerkind were physically rebuilt, the blank slates were thoroughly indoctrinated and trained intensely. What eventually emerged were Tigers, standing over eight-feet tall, with killing skills of the highest caliber and an unbreakable loyalty to the state. At least, that's what Malgato's masters thought.

They got the first part right.

Malgato dropped to all fours as her team padded along the water's edge. She inhaled the salt air, savoring the nuances of rotting crab and wet stone. The sand and pebbles here were gray and white instead of saffron, and massive sun-bleached logs were tossed everywhere. Her team was somewhat exposed, but their fur blended in well. Their armament, not so much. Major Malgato wasn't worried. Any viable area defense had been damaged or destroyed by the tectonic plate shift. Random round-eyes wouldn't be any trouble for her team; in fact, the barbaric humans would provide fleeting entertainment.

After half an hour, they reached the main shore and faded into the woods. The trees led up an incline to a massive plateau, one that stretched back into huge fields of salt grass. Jagged mountains filled the eastern horizon. Unfortunately, the team was not headed to the mountains; the major really liked mountains.

"Tigers, parallel the highway on the other side. We'll turn and hug the Hood Canal until we find Kitsap-Bangor Naval Base and secure it for the People's Army. After that, we are going to go exploring in the Republic of China's newest vassal state as our reward. Plenty of time to catch a few mice and play, perhaps look around those new mountains," the Major purred.

Everyone knew that *mice* was a code phrase for the ignorant humans that infested this beautiful place. Low happy rumbles rolled up and over Major Malgato as her team contemplated the thought. They entered the sea of salt grass without a ripple.

Her head slowly swayed back and forth across the vista as the Tigers slipped through the tall grass. A rabbit burst from hiding in front of her. Her right paw automatically slapped the rodent and broke its neck. Malgato pulled the carcass to her and sniffed it. She had heard of rabbits, but this was the first time she had encountered one—at least that she could remember. Her mind had so many holes in it, there wasn't much left of who she used to be.

The Major popped the fresh meat in her mouth and chewed. Tender. A lot of fur. She swallowed. Not very filling, but it made for a savory bite in a pinch. However, now she was in the mood for fresh kill, and this little tidbit had been just a tease.

She spit out a glob of fur. She would soon have her chance.

The Barton brothers, Don and Edgar, were not at all unhappy with the fall of civilization in their parts. They had always poached deer and elk, and eventually developed a bad reputation for stealing other people's crab pots with everything they contained. This was the lowest a man could sink in this part of the coast.

They were lazy miscreants who no longer had to hide their actions from the law, because there was none. Not anymore.

This night, the boys were lurking in the fields east of Sequim. They were riding all-terrain vehicles they had 'recovered' from the shattered remains of the local distributor. Each ATV had been outfitted with banks of light cannons and lots of places to hold weapons. They were all full. Don and Edgar were ambushing elk for the coming winter.

The high-intensity spotlights would momentarily paralyze the elk, giving the brothers enough time to mow down the graceful creatures with their new assault rifles, the land version of fishing with dynamite. The gun store had been their first stop after the massive quakes ended, of course.

The moon was playing hide and seek, mostly hiding. The brothers were passing a bottle of rye whiskey back and forth, as silent and alert as a human gets on the hunt. When the moon suddenly appeared, they could see a group of indistinct stubby elk flowing through the grasslands like they were silk. They were heading straight for the brothers!

Edgar dug his elbow into his brother's ribs. Don was reaching for his binoculars when the moonlight disappeared, leaving everything in shades of black velvet. There was something very strange about those elk, he thought, the proportions were way off, and they didn't move like herbivores…where did he put his night-vision stuff? He turned and dug into the vehicle's storage before eventually emerging with a night vision monocle. He turned it on and raised it to his right eye. The field transformed into glowing green pastels. There was something directly in front of him, closing in rapidly in complete silence. He yelped "Lights!" to his brother, who ignited the spotlights.

Don's guts went cold. The smell of salt burst onto the olfactory landscape. He began raising his assault weapon to confront the creature that was not an elk. It was a damned Tiger, standing almost eight feet tall on its back legs! Just proudly standing there smiling with all those teeth gleaming in the spotlights! And was that a fifty-caliber machine gun strapped to its back?

"You're going to make one hell of a rug," he said, with a courage born of stupidity and rye. Then something very large growled in his left ear. He froze and slowly turned to look. A massive Tiger head was nine centimeters from his face. Those teeth were much bigger up close. Much.

Then, not having used up all his stupidity yet, he let his left finger creep to the trigger of his assault weapon.

The Tiger bit off his left arm so cleanly that Don remained standing, at least for a blink. He was still trying to figure out how to fire his weapon without any fingers when something knocked him off his feet, leaving only one foot behind. He still didn't start screaming until several of the Tigers surrounded him and began playing with their food.

Edgar wasn't as lucky.

CHAPTER 17

The Mansion in the Woods

We made good time, running the Hood Canal bank on all fours while the pup riding my back shrieked happily and urged me to go faster. Rachel is a Wolf born to excel. But noisy, very noisy.

But now the rosy hint of day had begun creeping our way and we needed to find a place to go to ground. Soon.

"Eight, Ten, patrol left. Thirteen, Two, go right. Four, Nine and Eleven, cover our backs. Everyone else, just move out a bit, enlarge our sweep pattern. Five, Seven, and Six. you're point. Move out!" I ordered. Everyone followed their orders.

It was good to be pack.

Eight minutes later we had found one option, but it was too exposed, so we kept going, loping along in the shoreline ashes with the salt wind in our faces, on hunt for a refuge. This was the very definition of a good day!

We kept running into the sunrise in search of a temporary den. It wouldn't be long before we would be fully exposed in the light of day. Then Eight and Ten returned.

"We found a good place, big and well-hidden. There are nests of unwashed humans in part of the building," Eight reported. We all immediately changed course, endeavoring to move silently now. It was important that no one see us go to ground.

"Shh, Rachel, quiet walking time. You know what to do," I whispered over my shoulder as we moved through the burned-out village. She mimed zipping her mouth closed and settled in against my back. Apparently, she needed a lot of hugs, so I would always roll my head back to nuzzle her hair when she hugged me. This seemed to make her happy.

We continued moving inland and uphill, until we came to a very old mansion surrounded by untouched old-growth forest. The building itself was huge, a sort of log hunting lodge with Gothic wings and mossy roofs with crooked chimneys. The rambling structure was shades of ivory and the palest of yellows in the forest-filtered dawn's light. A glow showed in one second-story window, at the left end of the mansion. Everyone saw it, even the pup.

"Pull in closer now. Five, Seven, Six, you are point. Take us to the other wing of this monstrous place, far from the humans. Let's move," I said. We moved in silence to the side exterior stairs and began climbing the worn steps. We all seemed to need more sleep than before. The new life we'd dived into was much more demanding on our bodies and minds than our lives as mere caged Dogs. It was a long night, and it was definitely getting to be that time of the morning.

Twelve pushed little pieces of wire into the lock and the door clicked open. He stood back to let us in. We entered the second floor from a balcony strewn with broken glass and tree limbs. Inside, I immediately felt cut off from forest. There was very little light, and numerous dark holes in the floor, but we had no problem making our way to the staircase at the back of this wing. I could tell that the humans who built the place were scared of the forest from the way the hallways and rooms hid from it. *How very human, to close themselves off from the forest surrounding them*, I thought.

The staircase would have been difficult for a human to make out, but we Wolves have good eyesight. There were nests of rats and raccoons on the third floor, but nothing larger. Soon, we had found a good, defensible location with heavy doors and multiple exits, one leading outside. We naturally fell into a working rhythm as we established camp. Nobody felt the need to speak. Some of us dragged furniture and bookcases into casual fortifications while others set up sentry posts outside our refuge. Everybody else swabbed out the multi-story library we'd decided made a good place to lay our heads. That was when I noticed the fireplace and walked over to it.

We still talked about the barefoot man on the vids that made fire with a string and some branches. We had all wanted to try it, but we'd been on the move for a while now. This seemed like the perfect time!

"Five, Seven, Six, please go back and gather the tree limbs off the balcony with the broken glass. You will also be the first to try to make fire, but everyone will get a chance," I said. Five tossed me a quizzical look when he thought I wasn't looking. He was wondering why I was being nice to him. Good. Let him think on that.

Instead of how much he wants to be alpha.

Eight swept out the tile fireplace, and the chimney appeared to be clear. When Five and his guys got back, everyone clustered around Five as he sat on the floor in the early morning light pouring down through a high window, carefully shaving bark with an ebony talon. He tugged on it, and it broke. After thinking for a second, he began carefully shaving three bark pieces. Then he wove the pieces into a small rope and tied the ends onto his makeshift *bow*. Lots of tail wagging, and a couple of excited yelps that were quickly quieted. This was very exciting!

Rachel was excited about having a fire, too. Five carefully placed the pointed end of his fire stick in the tinder and attached his bow. Then he began sawing frantically as his audience watched, spellbound. A thin thread of smoke sailed upward, but the kindling shreds didn't catch. Five repositioned them and tried again.

A thought occurred to me.

"We're running short on our Licuado Protein shakes. We'll only have those in the mornings for now. But tonight, well… those raccoons looked fat and juicy. Not the same as venison, but there are a lot more of them, and they're just down the hall," I said. Lots more tail wagging, and I found my own mouth salivating at the idea of fresh meat after so long.

Then a small light bloomed in Five's paws and after some gentle Wolf breaths, it caught and fire blossomed in the branches piled in the fireplace, turning the dark wooded library into gleaming shades of gold and chocolate. Rachel appointed herself in charge of the fire and poked at it with sticks much more than was necessary.

"Five, take Two, Eleven, Thirteen, and Nine hunting, and bring back enough fresh meat for everybody. Don't make noise, humans move around a lot during the day," I ordered.

I moved over to lay in good-dog position next to the small human as she stabbed at the fire. It was a comfortable silence. Staring into the flames, I wondered if she still saw the same things as she did when we first met, when she lost her family and home in fire and smoke. I reached out a paw and ruffled her hair. She smiled softly and returned her gaze to the flames.

It wasn't long before a ruckus arose in the old house, with raccoons squealing and rats running noisily for their lives. One crash followed by another had me on my paws, in concern. I moved to the big door in time for it to swing open and five excited Wolves poured into the room lugging meaty carcasses in both paws. Five howls; the triumphant hunters were home with the meat.

Suddenly, I was centimeters from Five's bearded muzzle, glaring into his eyes. He glared back.

"What happened to no noise?" I demanded in a gravely low voice.

"I'm not scared of some stinking human pack," Five growled. Then he added, "like you," under his breath, but everyone heard him. Wolves have very good hearing.

I tore his throat open.

Leaning over him, I growled as he lay helpless before me, voiceless for the moment as his throat regenerated. He ritually offered me his neck in submission, but I left it alone to repair itself and walked back to the fireplace where Rachel was holding her arms around her knees tightly. The little human girl didn't look me in the eye, but she clearly had something to say. I waited silently.

"Did you have to hurt Five?" Rachel asked anxiously. "I don't like it when my pack fights." She was rocking from side to side.

I liked the "my pack" part. It meant she was beginning to understand what I had been telling her about it and her place among us. She was my cub now and needed to find her place in the pack hierarchy—to know herself. I moved a step closer to my daughter cub and answered her questions honestly.

"Yes, I had to. He challenged me as the alpha of the pack by showing contempt. I had to hurt him so he will remember what happens when he's being feral. I didn't kill him; he just needed a little chewing on. Wolves have been doing this for a long time. Five adds strength to the pack, but sometimes he wants to be alpha… to be me," I explained. We want to include cubs in everything and answer all their questions.

Humans lie and Wolves are above that.

"Are you going to bite *me,* if I'm bad?" she suddenly asked with a little uncertainly. I push my head down to rub Rachel's hair and sniff it loudly. She giggled nervously.

"Of course not! You are our pup. You were not born a Wolf, but you are a Wolf now, with a pack to protect you, always. We would never hurt a cub. We…" I paused to search for the right words, "cherish you, our only daughter. Things will get better, once we make it to the Hoh Rain Forest and can build a home in the woods. Once we don't have to hide from the Commander," I said carefully.

"Good. I don't want anybody to bite me and make blood come out," she stated with some relief. "Should I be mad at Five?" Rachel asked quietly, as she stabbed at the fire with a sharp stick.

"No, Rachel, he has learned his lesson. The pack is of one mind again," I explained.

"Good. I want everyone to be friends. I'm hungry," she said, changing the subject with a speed that made me a little dizzy.

"Do you want me to burn some of your meat for you? I know humans like it that way, even if you are a Wolf now," I asked. Rachel nodded at me twice, then withdrew into a world of fire and loss/sadness. I waited motionless for a moment, should she have more to say.

But she said nothing more.

I took several of the sharp sticks Rachel had been playing with, then picked up a raccoon roast and sliced off a long strip of meat. I quickly pierced the ribbon of roast five times with my talon and threaded it onto a stick. Then I leaned the stick over the glowing coals. One look at my cub convinced me, "I'll make four more." Everybody knew pups need plenty of meat to grow up big and strong. I could hear my pack agreeing in yips and snarls.

I growled, and everybody quieted down. The meat began to sizzle and pop as Rachel and I watched, entranced. It smelled pretty good for burned food.

Rachel was as captivated by the food cooking as I was. YouTube in real time!

I felt certain she was going to grow up to be a wonderful Wolf! We stuffed ourselves in celebration, hers burnt and mine raw. Afterward, we leaned back to enjoy a mild stupor of the superior sort.

"Hey—look at all these books! Want me to read one to you?" she languidly asked, waving an arm around at the shelves.

I said, "Yes," but then a sentry scrabbled into the room. Rolling to my feet immediately, I moved to meet him across the open area in the center of the library.

CHAPTER 18

No Reservations

"The humans are approaching. They smell sick and move jerkily. Lot of shotguns. Very noisy," Ten reported. I snarled, following with a sharp growl, the signal for an enemy attack. I sensed my pack focusing on me with an intensity known only to Wolves at war.

"Seven, Eleven, and One, guard the pup and den. Five, Nine, Two, right flank. Twelve, Ten, Four, on my left. Thirteen, Six, Eight. point. Go!" I ordered.

We quietly worked our way back, using every bit of cover we could find. The enemy was noisy and careless. We were not.

But they were toting a lot of firepower and appeared crazy aggressive, which was never a good combination. The smelly humans somehow knew we were close and were peeking around corners with their guns carelessly pointed our way. They reacted quickly for humans. Their scent had a bitter, chemical taint, and they reeked of smoke, cheap whiskey and metallic sweat—worse than Stinky, even. I wrinkled my nose in disgust and Ten sneezed.

A tall, greasy haired leader stepped confidently into the dim corridor and addressed us without any concern. Whatever strange chemical they'd been smoking had robbed them of all caution.

"You're going to have to pay rent like any other guests. Costs extra, 'cause you didn't make reservations," he said. All his men chuckled, and he continued, "It's eight meals a day for your group, or four meals and twenty shotgun shells. You can substitute a box of nine mil bullets for the shells if that's all you have, but the food is non-negotiable. If you can't make that price, well, your young women can work it off servicing our establishment. So, how would you like to pay? We don't have much patience for guests stiffing us," he added. I looked at him in amazement. He thought we were poor human refugees looking for a place to sleep! Humans have even worse eyesight than I had thought.

"Wait!" I said, stepping into the center of the corridor facing the twitchy leader of the odorous humans. He was sixteen meters away. I slowly walked his way, my bullpup shotgun held pointed down in my left hand, casually concealed by my coat and leg. I could hear some of my pack moving through the side rooms and halls, circling to come up behind the stinking predators.

The alpha just crocodile-smiled at me like a salesman pushing premium service at an unbelievable price on YouTube. He expected us to believe his lies. Even I could tell he was lying about only wanting a price to stay safe… that he intended to let us go. I found myself growling very low and bass but stopped myself before he heard me. He would realize the error of his ways soon enough, I thought. His skinny pack crowded around his side pointing barrels at us and staring at me with empty eyes.

"Where are the rest of you? Come on, I know there's at least five of you. Our bookworm counts good, and the kid's too scared to lie to me. And I'll know if you lie, too, buddy!

My, you're a big one! Maybe I could find a use for you later on! But first, payment!" he said with an outreached hand. His cold voice was surprisingly high.

I continued slowly towards him. When I was five meters from him, he acted.

"Ha! Idiot hipster. I hate hipsters!" he laughed. "Got you! Open fire!" he announced to his pack as he pointed his weapon at me and pulled the trigger.

I shook my head clear and phased into Flux.

All movement around me slows to a snail's crawl as my language processors are reassigned to perceiving the unfiltered world of base reality. Language ability falls from me in a brilliant light that never hurts my eyes. I see the unvarnished truth, and instinctively know how act on it.

The enemy is sunk in molasses, sliding down the time stream almost too slowly to perceive. I feel as if I have all the time in the world, and I do, when I'm in Flux. In base reality my hands are fast when everyone else's are mired in cold honey. I have time for precision of tactics that are both deadly and art.

I jump and slide to my right as I raise my shotgun, my torso still facing the pack of sick humans.-I actually get to the center of the gaping hole in the floor before gravity catches up. I am still firing as I fall through the hole down into the darkness. Every shot hits its target. Of course, I start with the tall greasy leader who likes frightening kids named Bookworm. The enemy has barely begun to wake up to the reality that we are not meat, but Wolves.

They never know what hits them.

There are fourteen of us, not five, but they don't know that yet. Odd mistake for a frightened human child to make. Maybe this bookworm scout was braver than his alpha realized.

I land downstairs in the middle of the decrepit second floor hall. I dash through the first door I see, entering a moldy, red-carpeted bedroom, and leap first to the unmade bed, then jump the rest of the way up through another hole in the ceiling. I squeeze through and am back on the third floor where the fighting is still going on.

I quickly reload, then leap out of a side door, back into the roaring chaos of battle. I jack shells into my bullpup and blow out the enemy's knees, time after time. They fall from my path like ferns to a weed-eater. I continue moving forward surrounded by my pack, blowing our way to peace, one bad guy at a time. We soon run out of targets and come to a stop, everyone panting in the smoke-filled moldy air.

We phase out of Flux… and looked around us. Lots of dead enemy. As we looted the bodies, I found myself thinking about the fight we'd just been through.

How did we know what to do? I wondered. Yes, the attuned awareness of our packmates was high, but there was so much more. This strange state of awareness not only slowed our perception of time, but also seemed to let knowledge spill into my mind from the time I was a human Marine. It was as if there were tiny memory fragments stuck in the cracks and fissures of my mind. When we're in Flux, everything worked much more efficiently. Maybe our memories were only walled up? Maybe some of it seeps through all the time, not just in a state of Flux. It could be how our hands know weapons and our minds knows military tactics, but not the names we were born with or who we loved.

CHAPTER 19

Bookworm

After we finished stripping the dead, my pack gathered around me at the top of the back stairs.

"Eleven, Nine, and Two, scout ahead, but be careful. We don't know how many humans this nest holds. There are probably more killers but there may be some non-combatants among them. Bring us back what we need to know… Quietly," I added, glancing at Five. His head lowered in shame. No one looked at him until our scouts returned.

"Once you get downstairs, the first two doors on the right enter the nest. On the other side of the hall is something full of terrible smells that hurt your nose and lots of glass things doing stuff. Containers of nasty smelling chemicals are scattered all over. I think that this is what Wolf hell must be like," Eleven said. We all looked at each other.

"What about the humans?" I gently prodded after a moment.

"Five female humans, four males, and a male pup. The adults all smell of gunpowder, rust, and metallic sweat. The males are spread out between the others and us, but are not even facing the doors," she said with a hint of disdain.

"Some kind of fight between the child and several of the women is all anyone can hear," Nine said. Two just nodded when I looked at her.

"Good job. Put away your guns. This is a job for bite and blade. Be very quiet. Move out," I ordered, as I crept down the staircase to the second floor surrounded by my pack.

We gathered at the sides of the two doors and carefully twisted the handles until something snapped. Six eased into one room at the same time as Eleven entered the other, and soon positioned themselves behind the two nearest men leaning on their shotguns. In the center of the room, all eyes were on a big angry woman shouting at a small brown woman. The smaller woman was protecting the small male pup, who was clutching a miniature book like Rachel clutches her dolly.

"He's a mouth who doesn't contribute anything of value. Dale wants you to sell him the boy. He comes through here next week for Martin's product and any kids. Bookworm goes then!" demanded the largest of the three angry women.

"Over my dead body," the smaller woman stated fiercely, bracing her feet for a fight. She flicked open a balisong knife in her right hand and looked the alpha female directly in the eyes. After a moment, the bigger woman broke the gaze and twisted to her right with her hand outstretched. When it came back it was holding a shotgun.

"Okay, deal!" she said as she blew a hole in her enemy.

I phased into Flux... My Wolves' blades creep in between ribs to still the gangsters' hearts. I leap to the small brown woman's slowly collapsing body, catch her and pick the little boy up in my other arm, spinning to shield them both with my body. Either the woman with the shotgun is faster than she has any right to be, or I stepped into it, but somehow, she shoots me in the shoulder.

It hurts like hell, and I suddenly encounter the downside of base reality; sometimes you want a little distance between reality and your perception. The pain stretches on forever without lessoning, and the snail's pace of my healing is so slow I can't even detect it. I continue my spin and return to the door, where I phase out of Flux… into the familiar ache of mundane reality. I knelt to set the boy down beside me and then gently laid the child's mother on the worn carpet. She was gone. I put my hand on the boy's back as he fell to cradle her undamaged head, heaving with silent sobs.

In the rest of the room, quiet reigned; the two remaining women had been disarmed and were sulking on a ratty couch, shooting deathly stares at the little boy when they thought we weren't looking. I sighed and rose to a stand. The buckshot fell from my closing wounds to bounce onto the floor. The bad females suddenly went pale as they realized what this meant.

I looked around the room one last time. This mean-spirited pack of humans were leaving nothing behind them but ruin and death. I watched as Eleven stroked the shaking boy's back before reaching down and picking him up to wrap him in a Wolf sized hug. Bookworm never made a sound, but his body screamed in tremors and locked muscles, in gritted teeth and involuntary convulsions, before he finally relaxed.

For some reason I didn't understand, I picked up the cub's mother's knife and secured it in my inner long-coat pocket as we left. We closed the doors quietly behind us and returned to the library.

Well, the bad humans had left one good thing behind—the pack had a new cub; traumatized, but he could be a good Wolf someday.

I think this new world is a little better now than it had been a while ago. Fewer bullies. Less mean. Maybe next time humans will think twice before abusing pups and their mothers.

Maybe.

CHAPTER 20

Cats and Mice

Tigers do not play well with others.

They are simply not pack creatures like Wolves. In fact, until the People's Army and their gene-master scientists stepped in, the Tiger's largest social unit was found in isolated territories run by a single alpha female, her wandering mate, and up to three young offspring.

Not these days.

The newly bio-engineered Tiger weighed in at over two-hundred kilos of sheer muscle, fur, teeth, and claws. They could never pass for humans or conceive of a reason to. The Tiger units were organized with a strict hierarchal command chain. One female officer, usually a major, had complete command over two special forces teams of four Tigers each, plus a tech and medic team of up to three more. To the human military forces, this didn't sound particularly impressive, at least at first.

Unless you listened very closely…

In the depths of the imperial city, it was whispered in the back halls of power that, "Twelve Tigerkind working together, could conquer any nation on earth." So far, the

Peoples Republic of China had only developed four fully-trained Tiger teams capable of a level of mayhem in battle that gave intelligent people nightmares. That broke down into two acquisition forces conquering foreign lands, and the other two back home to keep an eye on everyone. New math, Chinese style.

There was to be a new Chinese empire like those of old, built upon the loyal backs of the Tigers. Everyone thought it was a great idea. Nobody thought to ask the Tigers what they thought about it; after all—they were impure creatures born of the dilution of the master race's genes with tiger genes.

But the Tigerkin turned out not to be weak dilutions of some idealized human model, but hybrids with a hybrid's vigor. A stronger, larger, faster blend of the best of their ancestors' traits. All wrapped up in over two meters of tooth, muscle, and claw wielded by a wickedly intelligent mind.

"T is for trouble, terrible, and tigers," went the old nursery rhyme. Hidden truths in those words.

Of course, such power and size come with a cost, as does everything in this world. To function properly, Tigerkin required large amounts of a carnivorous diet rich in fat and protein. Multiply that by twelve team members, and you are going to need about seven deer, four cattle or twelve humans a day, just to keep them fed, which added up quickly.

It didn't matter. Regardless of the cost, they were worth it. In battle, the Tigers were unbeaten in all of Asia. Even more importantly, few people had even heard of them or what they were capable of. The Tigers liked to keep it that way by leaving no one alive on the battlefield.

Despite the deadliness of the Tigers, their Beijing masters saw only obedience in their politeness, and humbleness in their few words. They stressed loyalty to the party and state throughout the Tiger's extensive indoctrination and testing. Even in the People's Army, where all were supposed to be equal, the most powerful leaders ignored the threat and blindly assumed that only serfdom was displayed in their respectful bows.

Of course, they saw exactly what the Tigers wanted them to see.

This was because the Tigers not only know they were physically superior to mere humans but believed they were more intelligent as well. Add in that Tigers didn't really get that empathy thing and liked to play with their food, and on paper it was quite difficult to distinguish between a sociopathic serial-killer and an ordinary Tigerkin.

Tigers are just like that.

Edgar knew he probably stank of sweat, fear and worse, but he never took his eyes off the road or stopped driving. The caked, burgundy furrows in his forearm and calf weren't bleeding anymore, but he was getting just plain worn out from driving an ATV towing two trailers seven hours straight through the night. His adrenaline had given up and gone home for the night, and now Edgar felt completely exhausted. Somehow, he kept driving along the broken roadway, but soon he was going to have to stop.

Eventually, he was more tired than scared. That was when he let the ATV coast to a stop and dismounted awkwardly. Edgar just stood there for a few moments waiting… expecting to be killed. Then he became aware of the movement of large beasts and heard rumbling laughter with a gravelly voice right next to him.

However, that wasn't why he kept his eyes glued to his feet. He simply didn't want his gaze to catch any of the Tiger's flashing teeth—the length of his hand. Standing still made no sense, but Edgar wasn't exactly the sharpest tool in the box.

All night at least eight of the creatures had kept his vehicle surrounded as he drove, trotting up a calorie deficiency that was going to take a serious meat feast to re-balance. Edgar tried not to think about that. The fact was, this was more work than he'd done in years, and he could really use a break and a nip of rye or two.

Maybe a bottle.

CHAPTER 21

SpaghettiOs & Candy

The moon was growing fat, moonlight pouring down through the forest's gaps in light-falls of purist silver. I felt only a faint urge to howl. Wasn't time yet. I drew in a slow rib-stretching breath through my nose and let it trickle out my mouth. The purity of the night's scents laid down over cedar and fir were both invigorating and calming at the same time. We Wolves are forest creatures and thrive in these beautiful places. We were really enjoying this part of the journey to the promised land, the Hoh Rain Forest we'd learned about on YouTube.

I loved the way the ancient forest here came almost all the way down to the saltwater in a jagged wall of darkest emerald and deep shadow verdant. I was pleased that no one disturbed our passage or tried to waylay us and play cruel human games, even though we strode brazenly down the middle of the broken road.

There was a good quiet around us, full of soft night sounds and frog-song struts cut into bite-sized pieces by crickets and lesser bush musicians. The night was almost entirely free of humanity.

Then I thought of Rachel and Bookworm and knew that not all humans were the mean and greedy kind. Maybe it was time to adjust my thoughts a little.

Cubs do that to you.

Rachel rode my back in her harness, her cold nose snuggled into my neck as she watched our path over my shoulder. She was unusually quiet this evening but didn't seem sad. Maybe she was just happy to be back in these beautiful woods, as I was. Or maybe it was the awesome beauty of this shoreside road, as it skirted the cloud-clad mountains in the shining moonlight.

I was very glad to be away from that spooky old lodge, with its dark halls and nostril-searing chemicals. I glanced over at Eleven, who had a small human riding her back as well. Bookworm had not spoken yet but seemed alert and watchful. His platinum-blond hair blew out behind him, and his right hand cradled one of his pockets in which a poorly concealed book rested. I smiled into the sea-wind where the little boy couldn't see me. I didn't wish to frighten him.

We trotted in a loose diamond formation along the broken shoreline road, carrying our cubs or backpacks easily and moving in sync as only a Wolf pack can. The stars glared down in brilliant majesty, ruthlessly slicing the night into silver and black.

Later, around the middle of the night, we found ourselves jogging past dark residential units clustered tightly on the water's edge to our right. Not long after that, we came upon a small clump of the basic businesses a tiny hamlet requires. There were a grocery store, a bar, post office, two restaurants, and a Cannabis shop. The grocery store interested me. We needed more protein powder to fuel our muscles in lieu of our natural diet of fresh meat.

"Eight, Ten, and Thirteen, scout the exterior completely, including the roof. Two, Five, and Twelve, move inside to secure the entrance, and then we'll go from there. The rest of you spread out, around and up. We'll need your eyes to watch for trouble. This tiny town is too quiet. What happened to the inhabitants?" I wondered aloud. "Go," I added. They went.

The store was a poor imitation of the Safeway in Poulsbo. I looked around the interior in disappointment - no wing bar, narrow aisles, and dirty floors. It had been trashed and the dairy case was a wealth of interesting, if sour, aromas. I couldn't stomach a whiff of the meat department. That stuff was too far gone for even the hungriest of Wolves. I focused on the health merchandise aisles, and soon found a treasure trove of protein powder, amino acid supplements, and vitamin/mineral pills. It only took a few minutes to load everything into our backpacks before moving on to the battery section. Our laptops and cell phones were completely out of juice.

The battery kiosk was pretty picked over, but we were able to find some solar-charged lamps nearby that would allow us to charge everything back up to operational status. We also stocked up on disposable razors and some canned fish called tuna.

"Can I get down and go shopping, too?" asked Rachel.

I reached back and gently removed her from the harness and sat her on the dirty floor of the small-town store.

"What would you like to hunt for, cub?" I asked as I crouched down beside her, bringing my over-sized head to the little girl's height. "Would you like some help?" I added quietly.

"I need some new clothes, SpaghettiOs, and candy," Rachel declared with a shy smile. "Let's start with the candy," she suggested.

I nodded my head, sniffed her hair loudly, pretending that she was smelly, and pointed to the candy section. Rachel giggled and started making her way in the direction I had pointed. After several steps she halted, turned back to face Bookworm, and impatiently motioned for him to join her.

Eleven's eyes sought mine in silent question. I nodded slightly, and she took the cub from his safety harness and set him on the ground.

When the smaller boy got to her, Rachel took his hand and led the way to candy land. I lifted my chin at Eleven, and she took off after the cubs. Eleven seemed to be thoroughly enjoying them. Cubs have a way of sneaking into your heart when you aren't looking and that's good. Our pack should treasure its young.

A cold light of palest scarlet was creeping up into the horizon behind us. It was past time to find a place to hole up for the day and sleep. There just hadn't been any good choices on the road to Paradise tonight. Then my scouts returned to direct us to a ramshackle building on our right that hung partially out over the water. It was called *Oyster Bar and Grill.* I had no idea what an oyster was.

The bar was a truly strange place. One half of the building was filled with low stainless-steel sinks crammed with different sizes and shapes of stinking gray rocks. All the funny rocks were submerged underwater; the kind of water that made us throw up when we drank it. Seawater.

The air was rich with the smell of rancid fish and dead shellfish, but no sign of canned tuna. The other half of the bar and grill was a big room with a wooden u-shaped bar complete with bolted-down stools and a small kitchen that smelled of old grease and burnt meat. My mouth started watering. Protein shakes fuel the machine, but meat warms the hearts of Wolves. Been too long since we sank our teeth into warm, bloody meat… I yanked my mind back to the present and looked around me.

The problem with this place was there were a lot of windows that would allow anyone to look inside and see us. I glanced at Two for an answer and he led us out back. There was a flat roof that someone used to store rowboats where they were out of the way. Six or seven wooden boats were all resting upside-down on the solidly built platform. We quickly figured out that if you propped them up with pieces of driftwood, it was enough to provide a comfy concealed shelter that couldn't be detected from below. Five set up sentries, then after a quick dinner of protein shakes, we fell asleep in three warm piles of nodding Wolves.

It was a good night's day.

CHAPTER 22

The end and beginning of Henry Chen

"I don't know why the resistance claims to actually have Chinese members—we're here to protect our people! Well, that and expand the People's Republic's sphere of influence. These hairy barbarian creatures are fighting us tooth and nail over a burned-out wasteland!" Jun-Yi Feng observed as his eyes drifted across what used to be West Vancouver. In some places one couldn't even see remains of buildings due to the rubble from YJ-82KD ship's missile bombardment.

A foul ceiling of smoke, pulverized brick dust, and debris hung over the once-beautiful city like a particularly ugly shroud. Closer up it looked like one of Dante's levels of hell, but he had no interest in the scribblings of white men, and so the likeness escaped him.

Henry Chen crouched in the dubious shelter of Canard Boulevard's concrete walls, what was left of them, anyway. The continuous ship-to-shore missiles had methodically marched a destruction zone north and south, then creeping ever eastward towards Vancouver's downtown. The rain of fire and explosives pulverized apartment buildings and parking structures into an irritating grit that hung in the dust-choked air like razors.

Once, Henry had been a simple man who loved his wife and young daughter, enjoyed his job as lead chef in a respected regional restaurant, and thought life was about as good as it could get.

That was before the People's Navy decided to lend a helping hand. The earthquakes and fault line shifts had been bad enough. Then Henry's old country showed up and started blasting a mixed commercial and apartment neighborhood into dust and pebbles.

That was much worse.

The most terrible of day of his life had started normally enough. Henry had always gone to the fish market early to pick out the day's special, and this was his first visit since the quakes. If there were a few collapsed buildings and some meter-wide cracks in the ground, it didn't slow the pace of the market one bit. It had been three days since the earthquake tore up the western seaboard and life was getting back to a new kind of normal. Henry had bargained for a whole grouper, thinking about how he had missed the banter in the market and was relieved some things were still the same. The fish had weighed twenty-three kilos, but would yield fifteen kilos of delicious fillet, not to mention the other parts that formed the base of his famous 'two-day soup'.

Time moved at a different pace in the market, especially in those days, and before he had realized it, it was time to walk his daughter to second grade as he had done every day 'before'. He had lugged the fish to his car, which ran on fish oil instead of petrol—you could smell Henry coming a block away as the unmistakable scent of fresh fried fish rolled out from the old Mercedes in all directions.

There had been a new road closure in Henry's way, so he had decided to avoid the congestion by going a longer, roundabout route. Unfortunately, so had a few hundred other brave souls. He had been late.

It was the first day of classes since the earthquake. Henry's beloved wife had decided to walk his daughter, Lily, to school that day because Henry was taking so long. She had known that sometimes the restaurant was a little demanding. It had happened before, and she didn't mind. She was married to an almost famous chef.

That morning the television news channels remaining on air had been all worked up. Qianru had been drifting through the news channels like a bored man, which made her smile—Henry was never bored. Neither was she, for that matter. Both surviving Mandarin channels were full of Chinese government propaganda, but there were always a few Canadian ones that gave alternate views.

According to them, it sounded like the People's Republic of China had been *forced* to send troops to Canada to protect the sizable ex-patriot colony of ethnic Asians, who were being robbed and murdered by drunk white supremacists on the rampage. This was after suffering the earthquakes and tectonic shift! She had frowned. Even if somebody had to do something, she was pretty sure that the Peoples Navy was not the one to do it. She had wondered why she hadn't heard anything about this in the neighborhood or on the local news but then dismissed both the thought and the channel.

Of course, it hadn't mattered that no one actually requested or wanted the Peoples Republic of China's help. Many people here were part of the dual-wave diaspora from the recently subjugated territories of Hong Kong and Taiwan. And everybody remembered Tibet. The local community knew exactly what the Peoples Republic was capable of. She had flicked off the TV and put on her new favorite coat after one last look out the window for her husband.

That morning had been a bright, sunny day with just enough cold to make her enjoy the sun's warmth. The streets had been roughly cleared by the neighborhood, with everyone pitching in together. Her neighbors had agreed that if they waited for the city to do it, they'd still be waiting in the spring!

Lily had been chattering on, excited about seeing her friends at school again, and her mother had just been enjoying the morning as they walked. When they heard a whistling in the air, she had shielded her eyes just in time to see a blur coming at them. She had instinctively reached for Lily, who was turning to look at her mother in question. Then they were gone.

Henry had been too late.

He had knelt in the dust, cradling a battered piece of coat his wife had bought the week before. In his right hand was an empty scuffed shoe, Lily's favorite. He had raised his head and screamed to the heavens in pain, and it was a sound no one would ever forget, although they certainly tried.

When Henry had stood up after a timeless period, he had scrubbed his face clean of tears, and had started to get angry. Sailors from the Peoples Navy had slaughtered his wife and child, ethnic Chinese just like they were, without a second thought.

He had vehemently sworn there would be hell to pay. He would have one last mission before he could join his beloved family again in death. His family's killers were going to be put down like the mad dogs they were. Their ship too.

Henry's oath was something to be taken seriously, for he had once been a soldier.

Not a soldier's cook, or driver, or bureaucrat shuffling endless papers all day long. Henry was a fighting man. One that hailed from Wu Dang Mountain. Wu Dang is the birthplace of Tai Chi, the deadly fighting style of the emperor's bodyguards, the Imperial Guard, for close to four hundred years. Henry was a twelfth-generation warrior of Wu Dang Mountain.

Henry's uncle had begun training him in Wu Dang Xing Yi at four. At seven he began training in Tai Chi. At fourteen, his training progressed to Bagua Zang. At eighteen he joined the Peoples' Army of China to learn about guns and explosives. He also wanted to travel the world—preferably as far as he could from the only home he'd ever known.

He ended up traveling far beyond the empire and found great beauty and stupidity in unequal measures. Eventually, he even acquired some wisdom.

The problem was that nothing worthwhile comes without a price. He had found himself becoming increasingly edgy without the constant action of battle, a stimulus he was beginning to crave like a potent drug. Henry had always been anxious between deployments, but by the end of those days he had begun to feel uneasy in normal society when he wasn't on mission. It had become an addiction.

Until Mailiao.

The turning point in his life had started simply enough when he was twenty-nine. His team was sent in to disable defenses in the port city of Mailiao in Yunlin County, Taiwan. Henry's trouble started soon after his team achieved their mission, as they always did.

When the full invasion of Taiwan began, he saw things that cut into his stainless-steel heart, cruelties that no one should have to witness. The worst was when he saw Chinese slaughtering Chinese, all in the name of China. He began having a hard time telling the enemy apart from his fellow warriors! The madness of war had always been part of the job. He was a fighting man in a long line of warriors. He had done the hard things soldiers must do, but it had never made him feel sick before.

By the time he got back from deployment he had completely lost his desire for war in all its many forms. That was when he decided that it was time to find a new life, one that brought pleasure instead of pain and death. A new life far away from the People's Republic of China.

Stepping back from active duty, Henry became a combat instructor for his fellow elite teammates. He had long ago acquired the skills of modern weaponry and had become the deadliest of warriors in a demanding field.

He was thirty years old when he turned down another promotion in a long line of promotions and asked his girlfriend Qianru to marry him. He resigned his commission and together they fled to British Columbia to start a new life far from war and violence.

Henry wanted to create things, not kill them.

Henry leaned forward to peek around a shattered entryway on Canard Boulevard. After a moment he gave the go gesture for his team to cross what remained of the street. He crossed last, hugging the rebuilt AK-47 to his chest as he dashed to the next spot.

The Chinese Naval ground forces were letting the destroyer missile batteries do all the work. Laziness is weakness, and Henry just needed to figure out exactly where to deploy his small but rugged squad to take full advantage of that. He leaned forward from his shadowy perch to watch the patterns of falling destruction, searching for a way through the rough fields of rubble and brick.

"There!" ordered Henry, and his freedom fighters dashed for the gaping basement opening in a pile that used to be someone's business. The thick, masonry dust floating in the air camouflaged everyone's movement from the occasional enemy drones buzzing overhead. Henry Chin, former Special Forces instructor in the People's Army of China, went last.

His new team was less than a week old, and he had conducted most of their training under live enemy fire. His people learned quickly or not at all, but he still wanted to be able to cover everyone while being intently aware of his surroundings. He suddenly remembered Sifu blindfolding him when he was fourteen and instructing others in the class to attack him. He had somehow learned to see with his body and ears and nose. Not at first, but the bruises were strong incentive and he had learned. The old Henry would have smiled at the memory, but that was before he lost everything.

He squinted and peered through the dim storage room.

The cellar connected with a service corridor that was securely buried under the rubble of a once-nice hotel. Henry briefly remembered guest-cheffing there, back before his world ended. The memory tasted of dust in his mouth, as did all memories from back when life made sense.

He couldn't help thinking of his family, as he did a hundred times a day, but he had many things to do before he could join them, troops and a ship to kill before he could at last lay down his arms and rest. 'One last mission' had become his mantra and promise.

That was okay, Henry was a tireless worker. The people responsible for taking his wife's and daughter's lives were going to be paid in kind no matter how long it took. Henry had sworn it. A man of Wu Dang Mountain kept his word.

He snapped a new chem-light stick and took over point in its green glare, working his way through the choked passageway one step at a time. He was followed by his second, Elizabeth Adler, who was already an excellent shot from a family of hunters and would someday be a deadly warrior, if she could just get a little more control over her hatred. Not that Henry disagreed, but his fury was a frozen anger that allowed him to function efficiently.

Elizabeth's was a blast furnace always on the edge of spilling over and burning everything to the ground. Jayhon said she had been a carefree and happy university student before losing her entire family. Now she was neither.

Jayhon, his third, on the other hand, was methodically developing into a decent guerrilla fighter and had a surprisingly developed sense of tactics—he claimed that his thousands of hours excelling at video games was paying off. Henry just shook his head. Jayhon helped keep Elizabeth focused instead of taking crazy chances all the time. He had been a university film student, in the days before everything changed. Now there wasn't even a university anymore. Henry made them his squad leaders in the newly born resistance. With time, they all had potential to become leaders. If they survived.

Suddenly Henry looked up.

Then everything went black.

Chapter 23

The Blind Fisherman

I awoke when the horizon started bleeding crimson. Twilight hovered expectantly in the wings, anxious to take center stage. Meanwhile the last rays of day struggled for life, unwilling to relinquish the stage to night's cold grandeur.

The day simply had no interest in fading quietly into the dark night. I felt a shiver run down my spine as I watched the sky, there was a feeling of magic in the air, in this meeting between the two worlds. I felt a sense of untethered possibility as night came into its own.

I stood and took a slow chest-expanding breath of the night air and let it seep out my mouth in gentle breaths. Dead fish, saltwater, and humans. And whiskey. I growled so low only my pack could hear it. Drunk men. I took another nostril full.

Firs, warm creosote, rotting crabs; my pack, each with their own distinct scent that somehow merged into a mosaic of family; pine needles and dandelion greens, fetid fungi and even some deer scat. It was a magnificent symphony of scent. I felt my tail begin to wag and ruthlessly quieted it. The dignity of an alpha varied pack to pack, but I felt excited tail-wagging was not something a Wolf of my stature should do.

Then I heard the fisherman speak for the first time.

"You don't need to hide up there anymore, come home with me. You're all invited over for dinner," came out of the night from somewhere back in the dark waters to my right.

How could he even know we were here? I met the questioning looks of the pack and stood tall to peek over the edge of our nautical shelter. My pack joined me, crowding their way into view. Before us, a silver-haired man waving his arm in my general direction from a commercial fishing boat that softly bobbed up and down in the limpid saltwater. I raised my paw in return, but he didn't seem to see it.

"Dinner sounds good, but how did you even know we were here?" I asked. *Why aren't you afraid of bringing fifteen Wolves home?* was my unspoken thought.

A previously out of view adolescent girl with long blond hair patted the man on the shoulder and whispered, "We have to go. Riley's boys won't be happy if they find us here, Grandpa."

Wolves have very good hearing, so of course we heard her.

A crash and several men's voices rose up from the bar beneath us. Those must be Riley's boys. And they weren't saying anything nice, either. I stifled another growl. I didn't want to frighten the grandpa or teen. Besides, we were all hungry, and a meal that we didn't drink in a few seconds sounded wonderful. Even if our mysterious hosts burned it like humans usually did.

"Will we all fit on his boat?" I asked Eleven, but the silver-haired man also had the hearing of a Wolf.

"It will be tight but *come on*—We'd best be heading home, and my family's expecting you at the dinner table tonight. Won't do to keep them waiting," he said quietly.

Well, quiet for a human. His granddaughter helped him back the work boat closer to the dock, but I wasn't sure he needed her help. Grandpa seemed surprisingly perceptive. I nodded to my pack.

"We're coming," I replied. Everyone quickly donned backpacks or cubs, and silently dropped to the dock beneath us. As we approached the boat, the silver-haired man was easier to see in the barely born moonlight. I had found it strange that he didn't look our way, until I realized from the tilt of his head that he had been following our progress by ear.

Another crash and the strident sounds of drunks brawling rolled toward us from behind. No wonder the criminals downstairs hadn't noticed us! I lightly jumped into the boat and immediately moved out of the way of my pack as they bounded to my side. The cubs were silent, but I could feel Rachel and Bookworm focused on our hosts with laser intensity.

I suspect they trusted humans even less than I do.

The fisherman flicked a switch on the center console. A soft hum came from the back of the boat, and a light splashing of water signaled our withdrawal back into the inky waters of Hood Canal. Riley's boys never suspected a thing. We wouldn't be so lucky the next time they crossed our path.

There was something powerful in cruising through the warm night on a blacked-out boat, facing the slap of a sea wind, focused on an unknown destination. Even if we were heading into a trap, I felt strong and confident.

I also felt a sea-born calm in my bones; should everything go to hell like things had the last few days. I felt almost serene.

After twenty minutes we turned up into one of the myriad tributaries pouring into the Hood Canal. Our pace slowed, and the silver-haired man piloted the creek skillfully by ear and granddaughter. His navigation was impressive.

Eventually we ran ashore on a pebble beach that was crowded by dark forest. The landing area was well lit, and a small crowd of humans welcomed us with smiles and a friendliness we'd never experienced before.

A beautiful blond woman of indeterminate age, with *mother* written all over her, stood just inside an open door to a strange building decorated with driftwood and shells. There were very few straight lines in the organic weaving of bleached timber and stick and stone, but then there aren't many straight lines in nature either. Decorating is a human thing, which is what made this place so odd.

Shells lined a pathway to her, and I could tell this place had been built by many hands with love. The strange but simple beauty of it all was stunning to me. And the smells!

A dense scent lacework of burned food, wax candles, and fresh berries fought with spicy tomato, fish, and baking bread. All our noses were lifted in delight, and we followed the blind fisherman eagerly as he led us to the source of such wonders.

There were long wooden tables down the center of the room with shared benches made of split logs sanded smooth. Each raw pine table had room for four or five of us on each side and we just fit into four tables, humans and Wolves alike. Bundles of fat beeswax candles, hugged by carefully picked wildflower blossoms, threw a golden light on everything, and opulent piles of red plums and blackberries ran up the center of the table. It was a magical place to be, for Wolves in search of a home.

Lots of tail wagging.

A white wine was served, but Wolves have no taste for spoiled juice. Luckily our huge soup bowls were Wolf-sized, and heaps of long crisp baguettes graced the table with the

115

yeasty presence of the best bread we'd ever seen. Then I noticed none of our hosts were eating yet, while we had started digging in like, well, Wolves. I growled a short warning and all my Wolves suddenly started pretending that they hadn't really been up to anything. The humans politely pretended not to notice.

It was kind of nice. Not a normal Wolf/human thing, I suspected. But nice.

Then everyone turned to face the old fisherman at the end of the table and became silent. Except it was more than a simple cessation of noise; it was a stilling of spirit as well. It was a communal, inclusive listening that left no one out, not even Wolves. The fisherman began speaking, and the humans bowed their heads.

"Father of fishermen, please bless us, our families, our guests, and our enemies, that they may become our friends. Please bless this food. Please bless the children among us and our guests, who have come in out of the dark, that they might glimpse a hint of your Holy light. Please bless the fishermen and may our nets be ever full. Thank you for all you have given us, now and in the days to come. Amen."

Then the silver-haired fisherman raised his head to look at us and beamed a smile that made me feel all warm in a place I hadn't known was cold. I quickly decided that this blind man was not a presence to be disregarded. I smiled back, and somehow, he *saw my smile,* and his grin grew even larger.

"Dig in friends, you'll not see cioppino like this again anywhere short of the docks of San Francisco. We here are of the dunker's school of soup etiquette, so grab a loaf, butter it up, and start soaking up some of this scarlet ambrosia," the blind fisherman declared, holding up a baguette in his left hand and nodding it at us in rhythm with his words. Grandma poked him in the ribs, and he looked abashed for a moment, then attacked his soup and bread with zeal.

It was delicious in spite of being burnt, and these gentle people kept filling our bowls long after they had had their fill. Rachel sat beside me inhaling her food with such gusto that I realized we were going to have to learn how to burn food for her and Bookworm.

Casual conversations quietly sprang up between my Wolves and the blind fisherman's pack. One of the grandsons began playing something wild and arcane on a piano tucked up against the wall. Then some of the fisherman's granddaughters started singing, and we listened intently to this strange human art. Wolves usually only sing at full moons, and there is a sense of melancholy to it, not this… joy. (And this was nothing at all like those humans jumping around to bass thumps on YouTube). This singing made me want to join in even without the moon overhead.

Everyone was having a really good time, until the door was kicked in.

Bad men of low ilk poured into the room with all the subtlety of a fire hose fully opened, and my pack rose immediately to their paws, dining pleasure forgotten in the presence of such creatures.

We closed ranks, facing the door. The two small Wolves leapt into their harnesses to ride our backs in rapt silence as they studied how a Wolf goes to war. We were thirteen hulking Wolves in long coats, a wealth of shaggy hair, jacking shells into close-quarter weapons and un-safetying our pistols as we slowly rose to our feet and stepped away from the table with the fluid grace only packs are capable of.

Riley's men slowed to a glacial pace as uncertainty swept across their faces. Bullies never expect a victim to resist once dominated. We were a sizable, unknown factor, and didn't look like people you wanted to casually mess with. We inched into strategic positions, a single entity of many parts.

We were three meters away from the intruders, when the fisherman spoke.

"The house of the fisherman is open to all who are hungry in belly or soul. This is a place of peace and worship. Do not initiate violence, my new friends, but of course you are welcome to defend yourselves or your own. I only ask that you wait for the moment when the crux manifests, before offering Riley and his boys some of what they're so used to dishing out. If we must fight, then smite them hard and my family will leave the very ground behind us cleansed in fire and blood, as in ancient times," said the old fisherman.

Huh? I looked at Eleven for help in understanding such odd language. She shrugged, so I looked over my shoulder at Rachel. She leaned forward to whisper in my ear.

"I think he wants us to wait until he says so before we eat the bad men," she explained.

"Hello! Over here!" Riley demanded. All eyes swung his way. "Just here to collect the rent and see who your new crew is. All these newcomers are going to require a sizable increase in rent, you know!" he said in a flint-hard voice. His men chuckled and stared at the fisherman's family like they were freshly killed venison.

"But we already paid you just last week! We need everything we have left!" the fisherman's oldest son said. I suddenly noticed all the children and most of the women had vanished, leaving only Grandpa, the fisherman's daughter Tosh, her husband Lenny, her brother Typhon, and their teenage son Witboy. The teenager had a lot of anger in his bones; I don't think he liked the Rileys very much. I returned my gaze to the alpha of this mangy pack.

"Things have changed out there, not that you'd notice tucked safely away in my woods. No police left in these parts anymore. Game warden got shot a few days ago. You're lucky to have our protection. That is worth a lot right now, and I will evict you if you can't pay us what's due. Now, you'll pay another three hundred or you'll get out!" Riley shouted. His men made scary faces at us. Well, maybe they were scary for humans, but we were Wolves.

I exchanged a look with the fisherman's daughter Tosh, and an idea popped into my head.

"Eleven, give our two gold bars to these… *men,*" I ordered, and the gold miraculously appeared in her paws. I nodded and she walked forward to within two meters of Riley. Then she deliberately dropped the precious metal on the floor before contemptuously turning her back on him and returning to my side. Her tail was pushing up against her long coat in anger, but the humans never noticed. We hadn't seen humans being particularly observant, which this time worked in our favor.

Nobody moved as the gold rang on the tile floor for a few seconds.

Riley's eyes blazed with greed as he quickly crouched down and scooped up the small but heavy gold bars. He nodded his head to the door, and his men exited the room without a backwards glance.

"That should keep him happy for at least a few months!" said Tosh to her husband Lenny in relief. I held up my paw to quiet everyone. Wolves have very good hearing.

"I bet they have a lot more gold if they gave that up so easily!" I overheard one of Riley's boys say excitedly.

"Well, I think we should come back tomorrow night loaded for bear and seize everything these peasants have stashed away. What are they going to do? Call the police?" the boss said. His men chuckled at that. "We can get plenty for the young ones, too. Pass a message to Dale and let him know we'll have trading goods tomorrow night. Tell him to bring the good stuff this time," Riley ordered his henchmen.

I turned to face the old fisherman in the silent room. He had very good ears for a human, and I could tell he heard everything Riley and his boys said too. His sightless eyes swiveled to focus on me in question.

"Do you have any shovels?" I asked.

Chapter 24

Oyster Po'boys & Irish Gangsters

The blind fisherman and his clan already knew they could no longer stay in their home, and so without much talk, began immediately packing the household up. Didn't mean they didn't communicate; a hand on a shoulder here, or help lifting something there said more than words at times like these.

We had the fishing boat loaded with furniture, cooking gear, supplies, and even the piano, before dawn. The fisherman's extended family were all wedged in here and there, but nobody complained. In fact, no one was doing much speaking at all, which was kind of unusual for humans. Then the old fisherman stepped up on one of the crates that packed the deck and spoke.

"Father of Fishermen, please bless our journey and calm the waters before us. We didn't know when we got here that this place was not to be our permanent home, but now we know. We can't stay. We're leaving all this corruption and wickedness in our wake; we must be focused on the new home we will build in the rainforest our new friends have told us about. It's natural to be sad about leaving. Let the salt of our farewell tears fall into Hood Canal, where they will become one with the sea. Amen," the silver-haired preacher prayed.

Then the fishing boat eased back from the dock and began to fade into the gray haze of pre-dawn. The humans all raised their paws and shook them back and forth and showed us their teeth. I was pretty sure there were a few concealed a few tears as well. I looked over at Eleven for a clue, and then Rachel tugged on my ear for attention. I focused on our cub.

"They're waving good-bye. That means you should wave back, or else they'll think we're mad at them," she explained.

"Wave back at them, and show your teeth," I told my pack. Everyone awkwardly moved their paws back and forth over their heads. I guess we got it right, because they showed us their teeth again, as they disappeared into the morning fog.

After a bit, we returned to our labor. Rachel seemed quiet, and I wondered what effect spending time with good humans was having on her. She had been quiet ever since the fisherman's family had left. "Are you wishing you could've gone with them?" I asked. She just growled at me.

Just checking. Pack is pack.

During the long night we doggedly built earthworks three meters high encircling the entrances to the large building. A hedge of meter-long pointed stakes was sunk into the earthen wall's surface facing outward.

Sunrise came early in red grapefruit hues well-salted with yellow of all kinds. We remained on track preparing for the coming attack later that day.

Bookworm stopped by and passed me a big jug of cold water flavored with fresh-squeezed lime. Tasted wonderful after a long, dirty night of throwing up protective berms using only a half-dozen shovels, axes, and lots of sweat. I drank deep and smacked my chops once my thirst was sated. Sometimes the simple pleasures are the best.

He took back the jug, wiped off the top, and took it to the next Wolf. Never said a word. The cub would talk when he was ready. Wolves understand that these things take time. Little guy had been through a lot. But cubs are resilient; I was sure that someday he would make a good Wolf.

Shortly before midmorning, we retired inside the blind fishermen's house for a little snack, then sleep and safety. The fisherman's wife "grandma" had left some woven baskets stuffed with something called *Oyster Po'boys* and something else called *chocolate-chip cookies*. They were pretty good for burnt food.

We polished everything off, washed up, and piled into a heap of slumbering Wolves. Outside, our sentries watched over us as we slept that good sleep you sleep after a long night's labor is done.

In the mountains, the nights come suddenly, and this night had a shining three-quarter moon just waiting for us when we awoke. I exited the building to the rear and climbed to the roof.

The day before, we had marked an escape trail high in the trees, and our sentries were already up there watching for the trouble we knew was coming our way. Some of my Wolves joined me behind the crates piled on the roof, and we waited together in that solitary silence that comes upon you before battle.

Then a sentry hooted, and we returned our wandering thoughts to the present, although we'd never really left it. Everybody checked their weapons one last time and crawled into position. The plan was to first engage the enemy at a distance, then appear to retreat. I expected this to kick-in their chase instincts and draw them in closer.

We could hear Riley's boys long before we could see them, despite their attempts to be quiet. Our cubs were capable of much greater silence in movement than his rotten pack. I snarled low, so only my Wolves could hear. We watched Riley's gang enter the open space between the water and the big house. They slowed down as they noticed the work we'd done.

"Boss, I think those damned hipsters are helping out the fisherman. There's no easy way in!" someone said.

"Just means they're all hiding inside hoping we'll get scared and leave. Now we don't have to go to the trouble of rounding everyone up," Riley said confidently.

There was a moment of quiet after that, then one of my Wolves shot Riley in the chest.

Chapter 25

Gangster Trap

Everybody started shouting and shooting wildly.

If they accidentally shot one of their allies in all the chaos, well that was simply someone's bad luck. *Fog of war* covered a lot these days. Riley suddenly sat back up, cursing as only an angry Irishman can. He quickly grabbed his favorite assault rifle and began blowing holes through anything or anyone standing between him and the hipster who shot him. He always wore excellent body armor—guys like Riley don't have the luxury of taking chances. When you live a dangerous life, you have to take precautions.

"Fall back to the trees!" Riley snapped after missing his shots and turning to run. "Now!" he shouted, and the mass of low men hurried along between him and the gun-toting hipsters. The timing was not accidental, Riley needed the cover. It hurt getting shot, even if it didn't penetrate your body armor.

"Zeke, Harold, Marcus, ammo up and find a perch somewhere up in those trees behind us. Take out as many of those damned hairy hipsters you can, but don't miss. They move bloody fast," Riley ordered.

"Bill, Maurie, Tubby, circle around the building and find out if the back is guarded as well as the front. Don't try to go inside or anything; come back to me and report! Tubby, if you think Bill's getting lazy again, just shoot him, okay?" Riley hollered.

"Everyone else, spread out along the perimeter. You know what to do. First one to ask me a stupid question gets shot in the ass and won't be able to sit down for weeks," Riley threatened.

Nobody had any questions.

"The back entryway is the least secure. I don't think they had time to fortify it like the front and side entrances. This is a lot of work to go to unless they knew we were coming—maybe we have a chatty employee! I want to know how the hell they knew, Boss! Anyway, the trees are real thick right up to the door. Somebody put in a bunch of sharp stakes out in front of the door, so we'll have to approach from the left side. Easy peasy, Boss," Tubby reported.

Riley had a bad feeling about that. He looked over at the fortification of the front entrance. It had a precision to it that you only found in a soldier's work. It was so well built that it was literally unapproachable, if you wanted to live through the experience. He thought again about the rear entrance. It didn't make sense, unless the former soldiers only did part of the work. This sounded more like the work of the blind fisherman and his clan. This *was* their home, after all. You would expect them to work on it, too. Riley slowly nodded.

"Show me the rear entrance! Boys, ten of you remain here. Tubby, you're in charge! The rest of you come with me," he ordered.

The sunlight filtered down through the myriad branches of pine and fir in a soft emerald tone. As promised, the door was the weak point. Everyone clustered up to study it. No one noticed when a long arm with razor talons reached out and snatched the rearmost gangster. Or the next. Or the next.

Riley turned around to look over at the forest patch behind them. There should be about four more men with him! And where the hell was that screwup Bill? Then a hulking lumberjack leaned around a tree to face him, and bared big carnivore teeth in what Riley was sure wasn't a kindly grin. He startled, then quickly turned back towards the door to see if his men had seen him jump.

They hadn't. He sighed in relief and turned back around again just in time to see a brute snatch another one of his men and disappear. His man looked like a child in the hulking creature's arms! These guys were big! And maybe not entirely human, either. Riley had no idea what that would make them. He didn't believe in fairy tales and DC Comics. But then, *what were they*?

The one with the big teeth was nowhere to be seen. Riley pulled out a handful of grenades and removed their pins before hurtling the concussive bombs into the woods. He followed up by shooting his automatic weapon nonstop into the forest while shouting curses and periodically turning to glare at his men.

Everyone knew not to disappoint the boss when he was like this, so, they quickly opened fire on an unseen enemy and made up in quantity what they lacked in precision. Trees were starting to fall from the damage thousands of rounds inflicted on the innocent wood. When the grenades exploded, many more trees fell, but he still didn't see one of those… *things*. He retreated through the back door into the big dining room and looked around in shock at the empty room.

There was nothing there except some pine tables pushed up against the wall. The old fisherman and his clan had moved out.

Chapter 26

Raining Tiger

By the time the moon had crawled high overhead, the terrain began to change into clumps of flatland brush and spindly birch crowded together into impassible groves of ivory needles. We left the canal's borders to follow the highway route uphill at a distance from the road. Our progress slowed, but we kept moving forward. Time was measured by the moon's position overhead as we trotted across the monochrome night in tireless harmony. The moon was descending when I abruptly came alert, inhaling deeply and tasting the night air.

There was a rank scent coming up from the road below us and I wanted to gag.

Cats, really big cats, reeking of gun oil and copper and explosives, with scent tones screaming of human blood a few hours old.

I growled low and intense.

My pack stilled, noses lifted high to scent the enemy. Then everyone was growling, a low sub-woofer thrum that vibrated in our pelvic bones. These were no stray mountain panthers or random bobcats. These ugly scents were a twisted mélange of human and feline scent in copious quantities that shouted that there was a lot of bad cat out there.

I can't stand cats.

Whether it's Wolf thing, or a leftover scrap of my humanity, or just a really good survival trait, I think cats are nothing but trouble, and they don't even taste good. And for some reason these smelled really dangerous.

"Hold on; quiet walking now," I whispered over my shoulder to my cub. Rachel squeezed my neck in answer and held on tightly. We moved forward through the deathly quiet to the edge of the woods and came to a halt, focusing on an ATV that was moving far below us on the broken road, its trailers full of dead elk. The elk smelled really good, the upwind air currents delivering delicious meaty scents. My mouth began to water.

A single unhappy human with greasy hair and dark cat scratches on his face and arms drove the meat wagon. After a few seconds I started, realizing this wasn't a time to get distracted by the heavenly scent of all those fresh elk steaks. I searched for the giant cats beneath us and found four Tigers uncomfortably close, loosely surrounding the traveling fresh-meat parade. I automatically growled again and this time I was answered by a teeth-rattling snarl of challenge from down near the road.

Wonderful. They knew we were up here.

These snarling felines sounded either too close, or they were still far away and simply out massed us significantly. Maybe both. We Wolves weighed out around a hundred and fifty kilos, which I thought was just right for the superior design of our bodies. But these beasts sounded huge, I mean enormous!

Great. Big damned Cats.

129

"Fade back into the forest and regroup for sneaking up on the enemy. Now!" I ordered quietly. Wolves scattered to the winds and eased back into mother forest.

"New perimeter set and guarded. Now what?" asked Five.

For once, he didn't sound like he was challenging me, just asking for orders. I nodded back minutely, but I knew he'd see it. Not all language is noisy. Sometimes less is more.

Then I looked up.

"Prepare for battle. Incoming!" I announced as it started raining tigers.

Four powerfully built Tigers leapt down from the tree branches above us, meteoring through the starry night, intent upon punishing us in bloody splendor. Not all of us moved quickly enough; the first blood shed was ours. Those huge claws and teeth were deadly; it was a good thing we healed quickly!

We learned several things from the initial attack. First, once set upon a course the Tigerkind were very fast but had difficulty cornering or changing direction quickly because of their bulk. Second, all those massive muscles and claws tired quickly, so they were all about the opening attack. They couldn't afford to miss; they burned so many calories moving all that body weight that they ran out of energy fast.

But we are Wolves.

I phased into Flux… and the burden of language falls from me in a glare-less bright light. The shift into base reality slows the world around me to the pace of snails and I begin to process sensory input in unchewed bites.

An intuitive perception of the beginning fight draws my attention to the right place.

My primary target is the massive Tiger leaping from overhead to fall upon me. She is coming in from my left, four meters away and closing. She is huge. I briefly study the enemy as she inches through the air in my direction. She must be almost three meters of snow-white death, wielding clawed paws the size of dinner plates. Her hindquarters are massively muscled, designed for leaping, rather than running. Her teeth are more like ivory sabers than the ordinary fangs I expect. This is a creature designed to kill.

I perceive that she is evil incarnate, complete with a human's intelligence to direct her malignant attention.

When finally she gets here, I shoulder-check the Tigers right arm in a direction it wasn't designed to go. It barely budges. An instant later, Five hits the Tiger's back legs perfectly so they slide out behind her torso. Ten dashes by the Tiger's massive head, drawing black talons across its face and eyes. A scream of fury erupts from the Tiger's lungs. She twists, shooting out an arm to slice open Ten's back as he passes. Sixty percent of his liver and three entire ribs are dislodged in one fell swoop. He screams.

Both fighters continue in their established trajectories. Both instantly begin to heal, glaring at each other as they regain their feet.

Understanding floods me.

And I drop out of Flux.

Around me, Tigers and Wolves were stopping and taking stock of one another, reassessing the situation. The Tigers, were larger, more powerful alpha predators that also have nanites and could heal on a rapid scale—just like us. We were not unique in the world anymore. And they outweighed us, out-bulked us, and out-fanged us.

I was undeterred.

"When all else is equal, the larger opponents will usually win," I remembered from somewhere.

Whoever said that wasn't a Wolf.

A Tiger sprang at me from behind. I raised my head just in time to seize its throat and snap away a mouthful of fur

131

and a little blood, but I failed to get the right grip on the cat's throat.

But she sure did yowl with rage.

The Siberian Tiger rose to stand on her feet, nearly three meters of pissed-off beast. She studied me with an alien gaze, one that made my stomach go cold.

Then she flashed her fangs and watched closely for my reaction. If I had been human, I would've been afraid, but I just growled low and mean. Walking forward, I closed the distance between us.

I was watching for *her* reaction.

She was coldly amused, and not a bit intimidated by my aggression. And I'd used my best growl! Eleven abruptly snarled, louder than a scream, at her alpha—at me—in warning. All the Wolves heard her snarl and bolted in my direction.

I froze.

It's good to be pack.

I was foolishly seeking a one-on-one fight with a much larger, bigger-toothed animal, without backup. I guess chasing hatred can lead to places you don't want to go. You know, cat places.

Spinning to my left, I took off, as if the devil were on my trail—and she was. My Wolves weaved back and forth, trying to stay between their alpha and the Tiger. It was very difficult to outrun her. The massive Tiger tore forward in an unstoppable linear charge after us, and we appeared to be running away.

But we weren't.

We're not Dogs anymore.

We are Wolves.

We drew the Tiger into our formation and then, having isolated her, closed the trap. She was now completely surrounded by Wolves. She roared, spit out what sounded like curse words in a strange language, and lunged at me.

But we were agile and coordinated our gunfire to the Tiger's blind spot, the back of her neck. She reared up, unlimbered a full-automatic .762 caliber machine gun, and started blowing bullets in my general direction. She was wearing supple armor that shimmered at certain angles as our bullets struck her. It was quite beautiful, but not the effect we wanted.

Most days, the forest is a low noise environment, but this day its pines and hemlocks were rocking to the auditory onslaught. Shotguns and Gatling guns hammered wood like insane woodpeckers and the rhythmic pings of 00 buckshot sounded like hard rain on a sheet metal roof. Sometimes I found beauty in the strangest of places. I don't know if this is a good thing or a bad thing.

The Tiger closed in on me.

"Put away your guns and pull out your blades. This is going to be paws-on work," I ordered my pack. I pulled out my throwing knives with my left hand, and my Bowie with the other.

I shifted back into Flux.

Time stutters to a stop and I feel as if I have all the time in the world, in this space between the heartbeats. I intuitively know what to do. The Tiger hangs in midair, her forward movement barely discernible. I study the enemy.

In base reality, to know is to act.

I begin my spin, releasing the first of my throwing knives at the space the Tiger's eye would soon occupy. Then a second, so smoothly that it appears simultaneous with the first spinning blade.

The Tiger shifts, and the first thrown blade misses, but the second bursts her right eyeball like a water balloon. The third splits the leopard's grin; it sags into a frown with lots of blood and drool scattering. She screams in anger so powerful that I flinch for a second.

I tear out her throat in bright copper and scarlet. The droplets drift outward as I turn and seize the Tiger's neck from behind and rip its massive head clean off.

There's no coming back from that, no matter how many nanites are coursing through your veins. The body collapses beneath me as if boneless.

The death-scream of a packmate pierces the air and I stumble out of Flux.

It is Ten.

Three of the other Tigerkind had jumped him and were tugging on his legs. Then they suddenly ripped one off and closed in for the kill. Two of them buried their faces in Ten's belly while the other bit his head completely off.

I screamed in fury and charged, leading a rabid pack of furious Wolves.

The Tigers took one look and decided to rejoin their comrades down by the meat-wagon. We could have caught them, if it hadn't been for the lead hailstorm several Chinese full-auto machine-guns started laying down.

Tigers.

Next time was going to be different.

Chapter 27

The Hero

The Commander accepted the fresh cup of coffee and waited until the sailor was out of sight before he poured a little Irish whiskey in to sweeten the drink. He leaned back into his chair and studied his force's deployment for the hundredth time.

As soon as this Chinese business was dealt with, the rebuilding and repopulating of Kitsap-Bangor could begin. But for now, the Commander's submarines and ships were spread out in a steel wall between the Strait of Juan de Fuca and an inland passage by way of Hood Canal. The Chinese destroyers and frigates wouldn't be able to get anywhere near Kitsap-Bangor without being blown to pieces.

He hoped.

Any ships that could leave the shipyards had left by now, leaving behind only a skeleton crew of techs, engineers, and SEALs to man the now depopulated Kitsap-Bangor Naval Base. Those remaining were tasked with securing the sensitive areas, communications, and prohibiting unauthorized access to the armory and magazines. Orders were to destroy everything rather than allow the munitions to fall into enemy hands, even if this would probably leave a crater larger than a town filled with dirty seawater.

Unfortunately, the Peoples Republic aircraft carrier Jangsu had reached what remained of western Vancouver's harbor and not only settled in its forces around the aircraft carrier but had blockaded the Northwest Passage in steel as well. The Jangsu's forces had already taken possession of the southwest coast of British Columbia and were currently in the process of seizing the crown jewel of the mainland: Vancouver.

This didn't appear to be easy going; the people of Vancouver were instinctively working together and fighting like hell to defend their home, while the children and elderly were being evacuated into the mountains. Everyone else grabbed a gun and dug in. The Chinese *humanitarian* mission soon ground to a halt outside the city's downtown area, but this came at a high price in the only currency that counted— lives.

Small arms fire, chain saws, and hockey sticks were hardly a match for the heavily armed Chinese Navy sailors. These forces were well-practiced in subduing hostile populations, fresh from their successes in Taiwan and Hong Kong.

The mothers, fathers, and high school kids defending their city fired and fought their hearts out, but there simply wasn't enough ammo to maintain a battle of this magnitude. Everything but courage was beginning to run out. They were down to a handful of bullets and were giving those to the snipers. The desperate defenders helplessly watched the missile barrages methodically reducing entire neighborhoods to rubble and bone, and no one could stop the destruction. That didn't matter, the Vancouverites fought like hell for every centimeter of ground. At what felt like the last moment the new-born resistance located a cache of construction explosives and brainstormed about the most effective way of using them.

The invading forces had not expected this level of resistance from sedentary city dwellers and under-armed police. The Canadian's usual politeness had been mistaken for weakness by the Chinese invasion forces. They had been forced to use heavy handed methods to make up for their mistake. The entire city was being slowly destroyed, and that wasn't exactly the plan, as the big boys back in Beijing kept exclaiming in colorful language. It wasn't long before senior officers began disembarking from their warships and taking control of the ground forces.

General Zhong arrived on the scene as his troops were attempting to round up some noncombatants to motivate the enemy to lay down their arms. There weren't very many noncombatants, though, and those they had been captured were already wounded or dying. These Northerners were crazy!

That was when a young lady burst out from behind the defender's line and stumbled toward the enemy waving an arm over her head, clutching what appeared to be a well wrapped baby in the other arm.

The general had been expecting something like this and called, "Hold fire!" First, one would test the waters, then the floodgates would open, and mass civilian defectors would rush to surrender to his men. He'd seen it time after time. After all, the objective was not to slay everyone in sight, but to subdue a working population into one anxious to please their new overlords. He permitted the smallest of smiles as he watched the young mother hurrying his way.

He walked forward to meet her; maybe he could hurry this part along a little. Everybody on the other side would be watching how she was received; this was a delicate dance, and everyone had their part. He just hoped none of his men would screw it up. They weren't exactly happy with the resisting populace, and not at all used to going easy when their comrades were being shot at.

The general reached his forward line and stopped, heavily surrounded by his personal guard. He wasn't a fool; just because the city dwellers weren't currently firing didn't mean they wouldn't jump at the chance to take out a high-ranking officer. He waited until the trembling young woman clutching her baby arrived. His guards now surrounded her as well. Her head was bowed down in… Respect? Shame? Fear? Who knew what ran through this uncultured barbarian's mind! He stepped close enough to touch her.

Elizabeth Adler slowly raised her head until it was high. She was shaking with anger and loss, not fear. Her eyes finally met General Zhong's gaze full on.

"Welcome to Vancouver. This is for Henry," she said and detonated her *child*.

Elizabeth Adler took out four city blocks and over eight hundred enemy. Many of the refugees still exiting made it out, because of her sacrifice. This was the moment; the exact moment when the *battle* of Vancouver turned into the *siege* of Vancouver, current population eighty-six-thousand and dropping by the hour.

Commander Elwha and his men watched by high-altitude drone and listened impotently by the radio transmitter Elizabeth wore, witnessing everything real-time as it happened. This wasn't an easy thing to do. Everyone who witnessed this day would remember the name Elizabeth Adler for the rest of their lives. She immediately became the most beloved, if tragic, hero in Canadian history for her sacrifice.

"Men, I want to go help those heroes just like you, but we can't. It is a foreign country that has not asked for our help. We can't leave the route to our homes and families wide open for invasion. And we do not have the resources to declare war on the Chinese yet, not when they haven't messed with us. But if they do, everything changes." The commander said to his grim-faced staff.

After a beat he continued, "However, a little logistical help to my enemy's enemy, done quietly, might make a difference. Begin assembling teams to drop food, medical supplies, and some decent rifles with ammo," he continued.

"Seahawks. Low altitude drops. Get in touch with the resistance in Vancouver and arrange drop sites. If the ground and skies are clear, take the time to collect some of their wounded. Transfer the injured shipside, to our fleet," the Commander finished.

Later that night, the Commander reached out to Bangor's commanding officer, Marc Christensen. Marc was a hands-on kind of guy—he and five of his men were seamlessly lifting a ton of stopping power when the call came through. The Tier One SEAL leader was no stranger to war conditions, but still found himself spending as much time wrestling heavily weighted armored wedges into position as doing paperwork in the main command center. You just don't find *that* in many places in the world. But then Marc always had high expectations, and he made sure they were met.

"Meeting at Command at sixteen-hundred for recap and planning," he ordered by headset. That was twenty minutes from now—he still had enough time to get a few more wedges into place. He was having fun.

"Priority of hardening fortifications has been standard for the last fifteen years. Everybody knows the plan. Now tell me where we still need to cover …" he paused to leak a tiny smile, "our bases. Starting with tasks. Tech, report," he ordered.

139

"Fifteen years is a long time in the electronic front," the head tech guy reported. "My team leans unorthodox, because it's harder to predict, even in this dawning age of AI. We have Anti-EMP coverage for all five primary sites, and sixty-five percent of Class B and C structures are fully protected. My men and women duel hackers for fun. We can meet that threat, and Chinese Navy protocol is rigid. Our AI says we're good. Unless they bring the North Koreans; those guys are nasty. But we can do nasty, too. Viruses are still the main method of attack, so we have isolated ourselves by shutting down all phones and electronic media transfers. Official Navy encrypted communications continue. Thirteen hours until our defenses are titanium hard."

"Ops, report," Marc ordered.

Two hours later, they broke for dinner and still had a few minutes to hit the showers or change uniforms. Then back to their posts for the rest of the night. When they finally got relieved, everyone retired to the extensive below-ground bunkers. There were a few bunks intact, but most of the bunker was in serious need of repair and cleaning.

That was when the unbelievable happened. He woke up two hours later to hear the base was being scouted by Tigers! Damned Tigers! He intended to find whoever pulled this prank and give him something to occupy his time. Someone had to clean the latrines. Marc thought a toothbrush would be the classic tool for the job.

Marc had always been a traditionalist.

Chapter 28

The Darkest Night

We withdrew to the safety of the forest and withdrew up the mountain to lick our wounds. We gently carried Ten with us in spite of the fact that he was beyond all pain now, climbing for hours in shocked silence. Nobody spoke, but Rachel passed out hugs to her pack-mates in tear-tinged generosity. Bookworm was holding onto Eleven tightly, and I watched Eleven lean her head back to nuzzle our littlest cub a number of times as he rode her back in her harness.

Rachel was quickly becoming the heart of our pack, just as Seven was our tech Wolf and Five was my second. She fit perfectly into our family, filling a need we hadn't been aware of before we took in the orphan child and made her one of us.

But the pack was diminished. We were less than we were, and the empty place gnawed at all our guts. Our pack marched nonstop through the remaining night and day in numbed grief. We were now fourteen, not fifteen. Near sundown, we found a vacant cabin standing alone in the forest, and we buried Ten under a huge cairn of granite pieces out back.

The sun was lingering at that last moment of dusk. I stood looking at the huge pile of rocks that now concealed a member of my family.

It just didn't seem right to bury our fallen brother without acknowledgment of his value. The quiet of the pack demanded a solemn statement about Wolf Ten. I looked into the eyes of each of my Wolves, and then spoke the only words I knew for this kind of solemnity. I briefly wished the blind fisherman was here; he'd know exactly what to say. I didn't. But I had to try.

"Since my first memories, Ten has always been there beside me, beside all of us. Ten is pack, there are no better words. He went down fighting the good fight, defending the rest of us from those terrible creatures. The pack continues because of Ten's sacrifice. We will not lose that," I said. Lots of sad, slow tail wags, painful to see. Rachel stood solemnly beside me with her arm around Bookworm. Tears fell down her face, but not Bookworm's. But I could still see that he grieved with the rest of us, so I picked him up in one arm and Rachel in the other. I continued.

"Father of fisherman, please take our Ten into your arms and let him rest at last. Please bless those of us that remain, the cubs and the Wolves of our pack, and the blind fisherman's clan," I said, unable to imitate the fisherman and ask the Father to bless our enemies without choking.

I was firmly of the opinion that ripping the bloodthirsty Tigers into little pieces was the best of endings. I was also pretty sure the blind fisherman saw things differently.

I snarled and pointed overhead with my right paw at the moon.

It sat on the horizon, fat and full, shining down with a silver glare that ruthlessly sliced the night into black and silver. It called to me, and I answered with a long plaintive howl of pain and sadness billowing out of my heart. The pack joined me in song, and I knew why Wolf song always sounded so melancholy. Maybe a little hopeful, too. I saw Ten in my mind's eye, and sang my heart out, slow and sweet in that long harlequin night.

Someone made a fire in the fireplace of the cabin, and we all collapsed into a warm pile of Wolves. We took comfort in each other's physical presence as we crashed into unconsciousness, welcoming the oblivion of sleep with open paws.

It was a quiet ending for a terrible night.

Chapter 29

The Stag

A gentle rain steadily fell the evening after we buried Ten, but not much made it through the foliage. Instead of a hard rainfall, we were in a world of constant drippings heavy enough to soak our long coats but soft enough to avoid notice as they hit.

The chest-high ferns painted us in watercolors as we slipped past, paralleling the creek about seven meters up from the rocky creek bed. The towering tree trunks made traveling in a straight line impossible, but once we began following a game trail, the going was smoother.

The trees were massive, reaching so high they touched the sky. We couldn't even see the stars or moon through them. The forest was thickly carpeted in brown pine needles and vibrant green ferns exploded everywhere. The ground was very uneven, untouched by humans or their machines.

I couldn't help but notice that we walked a little less boldly. Knowing we were no longer the toughest predator in the Olympics was humbling.

We had nearly had our asses kicked by a handful of Tigers and we all felt shame over it. It had cost us one of our own—but it cost them one too, which was something of a consolation.

As we walked the game trail, I suddenly realized I was angrier at the Tigerkind than I was at the Commander who'd tortured and killed so many of us. I may have growled a little.

Rachel leaned forward from my back and whispered wetly in my ear.

"You're still mad at the scary tigers, aren't you?" she suggested. "Your muscles are hard like when you run." I growled and stuffed it down deep into a safe place. Rachel and the rest of my Wolves growled in solidarity, and I felt a little bit better.

It's good to be pack.

After an unmeasured period, we came over a crest and found ourselves overlooking a large alpine meadow. The moonlight poured down in platinum glory after so long in the dark forest. But that wasn't what grabbed our attention.

It was the deer.

Halfway down the meadow, a huge buck with a massive set of antlers stood watch over a doe and two young males with smaller antlers as they delicately dined on wildflower salad.

I immediately knew that this was what we needed, to embrace our inner Wolf by engaging in that most cherished of natural Wolf behavior—hunting deer.

This was therapy for Wolfkind.

I looked at my pack. Every Wolf, except maybe Rachel and Bookworm, was quivering in hyper-excitement. I spoke.

"Time to do what Wolves are born to do. But Wolves don't rush down the mountain and catch a single deer. Wolves sneak down the mountain and catch them all," I said. Tails wagged, even mine. Everyone began to disrobe. I motioned for the cubs to leave their clothes on.

"The deer would smell our human clothes and hear them rustling," I explained, "You don't have fur to protect you, so clothes are your fur." Cubs need to know everything, so they can grow up to be good Wolves.

"Two, Seven, Twelve, and Rachel, you're with me. We're going after the big male. Five, Eleven, One, Four, and Bookworm, you have one of the younger bucks. Six, Eight, Nine, and Thirteen, you have the other." I didn't mention the gaping hole in our pack, but we all felt it. We would have to ignore the pain that nanites can't repair.

We are Wolves.

I whispered, "silent walking," to Rachel and Eleven did the same to Bookworm. His eyes were so big I thought the deer would see them shining. We split into hunting groups and took different approaches. I took the left side, my team slowly creeping on all fours with our tails low through the meadow grass. The cubs lay flat on our backs without being told to. Five took the right side, and Six the middle. Fifteen minutes later we had flanked them, but the big male knew something was up. His head was held high, his nostrils flaring and his hindquarters trembling in anticipation. He knew there was a threat but wasn't sure of the direction. We had them trapped between Wolves on three sides and a cliff on the other, but they didn't know that yet.

We moved closer.

Now all the deer were dropping scat and looking around, eyes wide with fear. We crept a little closer and suddenly a many-horned antler swept by inches from my nose, and I quickly stepped back to avoid the deer's rack and the sharp hooves that followed. When I fell back it created an opening the stag immediately took advantage of. The great deer tore by and I felt the air in my teeth.

I took off right behind him, snapped at his hind leg and Rachel whooped in excitement, clinging to her harness as tightly as she could. I might have scratched his skin, but all I had was a mouthful of fur. I spit it out and leapt into a distance-eating gallop after the buck. A howl eased from my mouth and all my pack echoed it in delight.

I heard a rapid beat of yip and triumphant howls when Five took down his buck. I kept running as fast as I could and roared in support. I grew closer, and the buck glanced over its shoulder at us in confusion. He thought he was the fastest creature in his forest. He probably was before we showed up.

Seven and Twelve drew even with the running stag and I overtook them all at full speed. Two was so close on the big deer's heels that one cracked him in the head. Luckily, we heal very fast; within a few hoofbeats he was back in position.

Seven and Twelve dove for the great deer's front leg tendons while Two grabbed a hind foot in his mouth. I began a leap intuitively timed to take the stag down by the nose.

I almost missed my target due to Two's effectiveness in slowing down the stag from behind. I rotated my head twenty degrees and took the deer by the throat instead. I pulled it down halfway, sinking my teeth into its throat. Hot, rich blood shot into my mouth and I almost growled in pleasure. Using my inertia, I flipped, coming down on my back paws. Then I jumped to his back and rode him the rest of the way to the ground, worrying the back of his neck with my teeth.

We stood panting around the great deer, staring at all that fresh meat. Then I opened its belly and took the liver, which I shared with the cubs. Each Wolf respected pack hierarchy and waited their turn at the buffet line. I'd heard Six take down his buck earlier, so I knew everyone had plenty to eat. And we did; we spent the rest of the evening eating, napping and poking each other in their swollen bellies like cubs.

Once, we had been humans, Marines that no longer cared to live. Then we were Dogs, enslaved and caged. We had escaped from prison, but were damaged in spirit, longing for a home. We denied our human side, but it was there, wounded and hurting. We knew we were Wolves, but it was here, in this place, on this day… that we would become both human and Wolf in balance.

We were whole again.

Chapter 30

Hungry Tigers & The Boxer

When the ATV finally ran out of gas, the Tigerkind shared the meat formerly known as Edgar; what there was of it. Then they took off into the forest on all fours.

Major Malgato marched her Tigers at a ground eating stride, one they could keep up for about four hours. More than that and their bodies became self-devouring. All that deadly muscle and sinew had to be fed well. Or often.

The Major had kept her team from contact with the human pack predators and bald apes in general, so far this mission. She didn't intend to slow down for anything non-mission. Play time would take place after securing their objective. The Kitsap-Bangor Naval base.

However, feeding the troops as they traveled to the target was a different matter.

"Next human nest we come across, we will hunt vermin and glory in in their fresh meat. Go to hunting mode," she ordered her Tigers. Growls of acknowledgement were heard all around. Then everyone sunk into a deeper state of shared awareness, slipping into the quiet world of scent and sight, the *Stream*. The team faded into the wood's shadows, leaving no sign of their passing.

It was cool in the damp forest with light filtering down in strange and beautiful hues the Major had never encountered before. The forest creatures, big and small, never noticed the Tigers until it was too late. Then they were gone, and a collective shudder went through the forest fauna. It was a long time before the small notes of the woods were heard again.

Scout Bin whispered to the Major, reporting what they had found. She turned to her troops.

"Tigerkin! Fortified farm three hundred meters ahead. Multiple humans, big hyenas, a lot of guns. Five Combat specialists in front. Tech and Medical beside me. Three combat in rear. Move out!" Major Malgato ordered as she began softly padding in the direction of the nest. When she was close enough, the Major switched to stealth mode, a continuous slow creeping that few creatures could focus on. In a short time, they came to a primitive human road and all eyes turned to the scout.

Major Malgato yawned and all her Tigers froze; tigers yawn in high stress environments or when they're really angry. No one had to guess which one this was.

"If we do not have protocol, we do not have order. Without order we have chaos. There is a reason soldiers follow protocol; it covers everyone's ass and reinforces the chain of command," the Major softly explained. "What do we call them officially? Mice? NO!" the Major hissed. "And what kind of report includes the words 'Lot of metal, whatever it is'? Whatever it is?" Malgato hissed, then spun without warning to claw the right side of Scout Bin's face. Whiskers, cheek, eye, ear—all gone in one swipe of the dinner-plate sized paw.

Bin silently struggled back to his paws and ritually rolled over to offer his belly with his eyes turned away. His nanites were already busy rebuilding his face. The Major just turned her back on him and everyone proceeded as if the last two minutes hadn't occurred. Tigerkin are good at that.

They called it editing time.

"Ladders?" the Major chuffed. Bin nodded, squinting his eyes.

"The problem with ladders to your watchtower is that they're always there, for anybody to use," Malgato said. The Tigers licked their chops to keep from snarling their amusement.

They made use of the ladders.

One of the squad leaders, Ziming, scaled the exterior in seconds without making any detectable noise. Not hard for a Tigerkin when he stands upright. Or leaps.

The faint sound of a dropping body preceded the squad leader by only a few seconds. He joined the Major and then stepped back one pace in respect. He continued licking errant blood spots off his whiskers.

"Next," his commanding officer ordered, looking directly at the squad leader. Ziming almost smiled but instead stepped backwards and turned to lead the way to a side entrance to the main fortification. The squad leader only needed to put down a couple more humans to get there unseen. The Major and a third of the Major's team joined him quickly. Then Ziming's squad moved to cover the front door while Yu-Kui covered the back door.

The Major could hear shouting humans even before she entered the compound. The entrances to the large house were fortified with wooden stakes set into an earthen berm around the door. It was a good defensible position, had anyone been there to man it. Sloppy discipline, Major Malgato thought to herself. She gouged open the doorknob with a single talon.

151

Then he eased open the door and five 200-plus kilo Tigers slipped into the room without notice.

It wasn't that the room was empty, it wasn't. A throng of thirty or so human males circled two fighting males in the right part of the room. Four pine tables were shoved up against the wall on the left, and a doorway led to another room that smelled of cooked meat and cabbage.

The reason no one noticed was because of the noise the cheering humans produced. The fact that everyone in the room was completely trashed didn't hurt either. The crude humans shouted and loudly made bets in a circle around the brawling contestants. It was very noisy.

Discarded losers were piled up in front of the lower side-door to regain consciousness in the slight breeze. The view was from the stairwell lip was poor and the bald monkeys blocked the view. This fight was taking forever to decide. When Riley rang the round's end bell, the Major almost screamed in frustration. Instead, she reached out and tore off a forearm from the pile to munch on as she waited for the fight to begin again. The crowd never heard the scream of the newly-armless fighter in all the ruckus. The Major was disgusted. She couldn't see the contestants, just these loud vermin circling the brawl in the center of the room. When was one of these barbarians going to end the fight? That was when the Tigerkind would make their appearance and create a stampede out the other two doors, where Ziming and Yu-Kui's teams were waiting. This was turning out to be no challenge for her Tigers. The Major wanted to blood them before hitting Kitsap-Bangor Naval base. She bit angrily and discarded a fist.

Then, her patience expended, she stood fully upright, nearly three meters of she-Tiger, and snarled. Her Tigerkin leapt high over the pile of sleeping fighters to fall upon the screaming and gesturing spectator's backs. Then they broke each man's neck with a snap of their powerful jaws, before moving on to the next gangster's back. They took six worthless lives before anyone noticed.

That was when things really got crazy. It was every man for himself, except Tubby and Maurice. They defended their boss, falling back behind Riley as he made a run for the back door. Every other man was scrambling for the nearer, front door. They piled up at the entrance, fighting fiercely to get out the door everybody else was trying to get through. It was mass confusion until gangsters started flying out the door like watermelon seeds. Ziming and his Tigerkin were waiting, of course, to catch dinner for everybody.

Back inside, it took the two dazed fighters a little longer to notice they weren't the center of attention anymore. One of the contestants froze upon seeing a Tiger coming his way, but his opponent just took the opportunity to knee him in the kidney and grab him in a headlock from behind. The stunned fighter was halfway to dreamland when something very large chuckled in the winner's ear, low and rumbly. He slowly turned his head to face an actual Tiger, centimeters from his face. He let the other duelist fall to the ground.

"I'm a fighter. I go down fighting," he announced before socking Scout Bin as hard as he could in the nose. He was very good at hitting, just not so good with the thinking ahead part. Bin screamed, pulling his head back and showering everyone in droplets of fresh Tiger blood. Then he took the fighter by the neck and shook him.

By now, Riley had reached the back door. He was in full motion when he burst open the back door to toss a grenade to each side, before ducking back inside to avoid the blast wave. He seized the opportunity to grab his favorite M-16 and a few toys along with Tubby and Maurice. Then he nodded to his boys and kicked the door back open to exit while the three hosed the waiting Tigers with steel-jacketed bullets. They kept moving forward and firing until only three of the huge Tigers were still on their feet, but these guys were

153

tough! Confused, he saw a fallen Tiger's wounds slowly close and spit out his bullets. As the Tiger got back to its feet, Riley's adrenaline spiked higher. The world slowed a bit as he sped up.

Riley and his boys had killed all manners of people, and local game as well, but he'd never faced any adversary like this. He dropped his assault rifle on its tether and reached behind his back to pull out a huge shotgun with a drum magazine. It was loaded with lead slugs capable of taking down an elephant. Riley knew this for a fact; an idiot Circus owner had reneged on his debts, and he had done what he had to.

The Major sneered at Scout Bin and returned to her bloody business, cleansing this foul nest of humans. She plucked a squirming human from the crowd jammed at the front door. It squealed, so the Major brought the suddenly sober human close to her jaws before roaring. It fainted and she passed it back before moving on to the next barbarian. She had noticed a few humans escaping out the back door, but the Major let them go. The other Tigers deserved a little fun, too.

Riley and his boys were on a hell march to his pickup truck seventeen meters away. He leaned into the recoil and never stopped moving to his objective. As he concentrated his aim on first one Tiger and then the others, holes the size of his fist began appearing in the furious creatures. The other Tigers continued firing back at them in a deafening firefight.

Then the four Tigers on their feet became three, as an under-gunned Tiger lost his entire head and most of his shoulders. The other Tigers quickly spun into the dubious safety of a tin shed wall, before crawling for better cover. They were cursing in Chinese, but Riley only picked up

"NATO 552's" and grinned. It was called 'Barbie-doll ammo' for a reason[1].

Riley made it to the pickup and quickly reached behind the seat to pull out a grenade launcher armed with incendiary shells as Tubby and Maurice piled into the dubious shelter of the truck. Riley laid down some more cover fire and jumped into the driver's seat, passing the smoking launcher to Tubby, who then leaned out the window and enthusiastically lit up the parking lot. The boss pushed start and tore out of there in his custom armored one-ton. Successful criminals don't take chances, too many threats out there already. Riley always had an escape plan. And lots of big guns stashed here and there. You do what you have to do to survive.

---

[1] John Ringo, "Under a Graveyard Sky"

155

Chapter 31

Prisoner

First, he became aware of the cold, and then realized he was shaking uncontrollably. The next thing he became aware of was the smell. He groaned. Hospitals smell the same the world over. Not what he wanted to wake up to, but he did.

It was bright. A lot of stainless-steel. Gentle rolling movement like... a ship. Henry tried to clear his head and began looking around. English, not Chinese. There were empty patches on the walls where things like flags and insignia usually go. Nowhere did it say USA or Canada or United Kingdom. So... something else.

His chest hurt. He couldn't feel his right leg.

He heard footsteps ring on the metal deck outside his room and immediately shut his eyes, playing dead to the world. The door opened. Light flooded in, then not as much as someone came through the doorway. He smelled a woman's perfume, lightly applied, mixed with bleach and gun oil. There was a smidgen of salt in the breeze from the door opening. Navy medic or doctor.

His deductions proved true. She began taking his vitals.

"You don't need to pretend to be asleep; I'm not a threat," she said casually, releasing the blood pressure clamp from his arm.

Henry opened his eyes and rose to a sitting position. He nodded politely at the…doctor? Nurse? She had a stethoscope around her neck, so she was probably a doctor. He waited for her to speak, worried about guessing wrong. It's a bad idea to anger the person healing you.

"I'm Doctor Mead. Do you know what the date is?" she asked quietly in English.

"Not really," Henry answered. "Sometime after the missiles rained down and took my family," he solemnly added. This was the first time he had spoken those terrible words.

"Do you know where you are now?" she continued, methodically marking things off on a form. She peeked at him over the document. She was analyzing his responses, probably checking for brain damage. Medics and doctors usually did that, in his experience.

"In the medic bay of a former American ship deployed somewhere in the vicinity of Vancouver, B.C.," he answered.

"Yes, that's right. You were medivacked out of West Vancouver by an MH-60 Seahawk helicopter after you were injured by a missile. Next time, just run like the rest of us. Still, everyone here thinks you resistance fighters are heroes and wishes they were able to help," she said, finally meeting his eyes. After a moment, Henry leaned back and allowed his eyes to close. He felt exhausted and didn't have to fake the deep sleep that followed.

Over the next few days his doctor proved to be good company for a badly injured man, as long as they avoided the subject of the invasion. Doctor Mead's dry wit couldn't be hidden behind protocol and regulation conversations. It just oozed out when she wasn't paying attention, and maybe sometimes got her in a little hot water, but what the hell.

It was morning on his third day aboard. Henry was listening carefully as she explained his chart and injuries. He was a little surprised to be alive.

"Left kidney and liver are damaged, but healing. Broken right arm and nose. Fourteen broken bones in your right foot and ankle. Torn ligament and cartilage damage on right knee; doctors already operated. You will regain full use of your right leg with time and therapy," the doc explained.

Henry didn't let his disdain show. American physical therapy when he had a thousand years of study of the human body distilled into Wu Dang Tai Chi and Chi Gong?

But she wasn't finished.

"Missing right ear, but your hearing is still fine. You're going to have extensive scarring in the area. From your examination, this is not a concern. Over fifteen percent of your body is covered in scar tissue and healed wounds. Vancouver wasn't the first place you fought the good fight, was it? Never mind; not my business," she said before he could answer.

"Does this ship have access to the GPS data on the attack forces in the initial missile attack launched on Vancouver?" he asked, after a pause. Her face went sad with understanding, but she just hung his file back up and said, "Do you really need to see it?"

He just nodded. As a man who had never cried in front of a stranger, Henry was in serious danger of leaking a little around the eyes, but he didn't. Instead, he directed his gaze inside, beginning the ceaseless circle of embryonic breathing. It really got the Chi going, which both calmed and focused him. He had a ship to sink and sailors to kill. That was the mission—not making friends with a navy doctor.

He didn't appear to notice when she left the room, but Doctor Mead had a feeling he noticed everything.

Wasn't her first time fighting the good fight either.

159

Chapter 32

In the Forests of the Night

Major Malgato studied Kitsap-Bangor's lonely docks, populated only by ghosts and ships too damaged to immediately salvage. She couldn't see a single moving figure. This was going to be much simpler than she had expected.

Overall, these pale northerners were a complete disappointment. But where were all the submarines? Intel said this was the largest concentration of subs on the entire west coast! Where were all the Tridents?

"Squad leaders, report!" she ordered by command circuit.

Ziming spoke first, "Scouted waterside perimeter of Bangor. Extensive damage to buildings and fence. The dry dock is completely destroyed. No sign of humans yet. I believe this is the primary route for us. *Hhuff.*"

Squad leader Yu-Kui spoke next, "Scouted the middle of this land bridge. Perimeter fencing is down in many places. Majority of fortifications are in shambles. No one is guarding the main gate, and it's lacking an intact access road. Many entry points, but no sign of dead, so someone was around to bury the bodies. Any forces that remain alive will have concentrated into a smaller and more easily defended territory. Suggest focusing on the area between my party and Ziming's location. *Hhuff*."

The Major contemplated the situation and decided to take the waterside route along Hood Canal.

"Ziming, map out any human nests, armory bunkers, or signs of radiation, but don't engage the enemy. Once I join you on the waterfront, we will proceed east to the interior of the base. We'll co-ordinate simultaneous attacks on the main infestation from both east and west. Check gear and load up. Won't be long now until the mission is achieved and we're free to explore this beautiful land," the Major ordered. She was down two weaklings, which was unexpected considering the cause. A rare few of the humans were almost competent in a fight. It didn't matter—she still had ten Tigers capable of anything, certainly capable of handling whatever these humans came up with.

The damage to the base was shocking. A massive white concrete structure had cracked open like an egg, spilling an entire aircraft Carrier onto the ground in useless fragments, the smallest of which was the size of a large house. The Major had never seen anything like it in her life, not that she remembered much before her life as a Tiger had begun a couple of years before.

Scout Bin spoke up, "Have encountered a hardened defensive structure crawling with big guns and barbarians. Enemy is firmly entrenched. Looks like this is an outlying fort. One of several. I suspect that there are tunnels running back to the main bunkers and command center. Somebody went to a lot of work to fortify this place. *Hhuff*," came over the command circuit.

"Confirmed. We've come across two more. So, four outposts, and one big ant hill. Spread out and scout all the way around this place. Two squads go Northwest. Remaining

161

Squad Southeast. Main party will perpetrate interior with me to get a better look at the defenses. *Hhuff*!" rumbled the Major.

"Contact with the enemy," reported Squad leader Yu-Kui.

Navy Marines were swarming to their preselected firing perches along the top of the fortifications. Humans couldn't usually see in the dark, but night vision tech had been around for decades. They could probably see her too. Yu-Kui lowered herself deep in the uncut grass and went stealth, moving forward at a crawl that most creatures had difficulty perceiving. She needed more Intel. Maybe she should capture one and bring it back for the Major to interrogate.

Navy SEALs are extremely perceptive, with bodies and senses honed to perfection. They always achieve their mission. But these Seals' senses were confused. A huge Tiger moving like an elite, special forces agent, was coming right at them at speed. It had a huge head with fangs longer than dive knife's blade! It quickly merged with the tall grass, but it massed at least two-hundred-kilos, most likely more. The Tiger appeared to have been wearing a striped military harness, full of pouches probably stuffed with the kind of things a soldier finds handy. Dual pistols, three rifles or shotguns strapped across its long, striped body. Other stuff they couldn't make out before it vanished.

Everyone knew it hadn't gone away, and the quiet as the SEALs listened hard for the enemy was profound. They waited behind a barrier made of heavily weighted armored wedges set in a log cabin style, rising seven meters high and layered three deep. The angles of the barrier were designed to deflect projectiles. The outer walls protected an interior steel and concrete command room with floor exits into the tunnel system.

There were twelve men on the walls, three per side, ears tilted to the night. Normal night sounds were absent, which meant that something big and dangerous was close by. They just didn't realize how close. It was over the wall and had snatched a guy before he knew what hit him.

The night erupted in gunfire. But the Tiger was already back over the wall with its intended victim.

What the Tiger didn't know was that SEALs are simply not victim material. Despite having his right arm bit off at the bicep, the navy man blew out the Tiger's neck with a 10-millimeter bullet barrage fired so fast that it sounded like one continuous sound. The Tiger couldn't scream with anger because it no longer had a throat, but the SEAL had no trouble reading it in the predator's body. He hit the ground and quickly rolled away as his team scorched the earth behind him in fire and fury. Once the injured man had been retrieved, they sent a team to Armory Twenty-Two.

They were going to need bigger guns. A lot of them.

Chapter 33

Night Sea Delirium

Henry looked up from the book he was reading when Dr. Mead entered the sick bay. Usually she was smiling, but today she just looked determined. She was holding a brown envelope in her right hand.

Henry became alert.

"This wasn't easy to come by, but if it will help you find closure then it was worth it," she said. Her brow was slightly furrowed, but she relaxed when Henry didn't show any emotion. She handed him the envelope and picked up his chart, reading it and casting occasional glances his way.

"Thank you, Doctor. This means everything to me," he said. Then he carefully put it under his pillow. The rest of the day progressed as it had the previous three days. Henry had been healing quickly, but until this day he had not been fit for interrogation.

From here on, everything was going to change. Henry did not intend to be here for the questioning waiting for him come morning. He watched as the doctor left the ward.

At twenty-three hundred, Henry carefully finished wrapping the GPS chart in waterproofing, taped it to his belly and slipped out into the corridor. He pulled a life preserver off the wall as he passed and wrapped it in a dark gray jacket from a peg on the wall. He had an idea of where to look for diving gear and was lucky enough to find a wetsuit. Once on deck he confirmed his target by the distant lights on shore and then wasted no time stealthily making his way into the inky black water.

It was cold.

He had trained his body to ignore such minor discomforts, but that was a decade ago. Henry tucked his concealed life preserver under his chest and began paddling the long journey to shore. He expected to swim it in under four hours. The shore lights hadn't been that far away.

After hours in the freezing saltwater, even in a wetsuit Henry's kidneys were throbbing like they were passing glass and he couldn't feel his right leg, but maybe that was a blessing. He found himself imagining hugging his much-loved wife and daughter tightly in his arms. He took the time to be aware of every smidgen of detail as he recreated the perfect memory in his mind. He stopped feeling the cold. Somewhere deep inside, he knew he was in bad shape, but he refused to relinquish hold of his loved ones. He missed them so much. He didn't want to go back to that throbbing world of pain and cold. He was tired and wanted to rest.

But duty, the mission, and his oath must come first.

Henry came awake burning with rage, wrapped in an icy body he barely recognized. He had sailors and a ship to kill. Now he knew the name of the ship that launched the first missile, the one that killed his family. The Jangsu. That was where he'd find the sailors, too. He couldn't rest now. He began stroking east, using the night sky for guidance. He couldn't see the lights on shore anymore.

He slid through the black salt waves in the faint starlight until he lost the ability to tell he was even moving.

Henry felt like he was floating in space, marooned in time unknowable. He woke up tangled in something with a bright light shining in his face.

"He's still alive, Grandpa! We got here in time," came the lilting voice of a little girl about Lily's age. Henry's eyes were tightly shut to the blinding light. He felt himself being gently carried into a warm steel room. It was noisy with a lot of people talking at the same time. Fishing boat from the smell.

The next time he opened his eyes, a man with a black beard and kind eyes was giving him sips of hot sweetened tea. It tasted wonderful. He was tucked into a narrow berth where he was layered in wool blankets padded with warm water bottles. His eyes were closing again.

"We have to get your core temperature back up where it's supposed to be. How long were you in the water?" asked the man "Never mind. You can tell me later. I'm Lenny. Guess I'm kind of used to being around the same people all the time. Didn't mean to be rude," Lenny said with a wry smile.

"Since midnight," Henry answered. He had to will his teeth to stop chattering. Five hours? It could have been five days for all he knew. Time runs different out there.

"I need to get back topside; will you be alright for a bit?" Lenny asked, watching Henry closely to make sure he was, indeed, okay.

"I'll be fine. Go do what you need to. And Lenny, thank you," Henry said. Then he closed his eyes and fell into the warm dusk of dream, out like a light. Lenny smiled, grabbed his wet weather gear and was out the door just as fast.

Chapter 34

Neah Bay

The blind fisherman's son-in-law Lenny noted their navigational location and frowned.

"We're further west than we realized. We'll be rounding Cape Alava at Neah Bay and entering the Pacific before dawn. We need to batten everything down and get the little ones below deck before then. Good news is that this places us two days from the river to the Hoh Rain Forest. Odd thing is—how did we find the poor guy in the water if we weren't where we were supposed to be?" asked Lenny.

"We *were* where we were supposed to be. We just weren't where we thought we were," Grandpa explained. Then he laughed and walked forward to put his hands on the wheel. The shore-side window into the cockpit was always open and the blind fisherman pushed his face into the rich wind. Silver firs and Ponderosa Pine blowing in from two-plus thousand meters in elevation, campfire, salt grass and hemlock told him the neighborhood. The faint whirl of the wind power generators further down the Pacific coast told him his position.

"We'll be rounding the point and going into choppy seas in twenty minutes. Granddaughters, batten down the kitchen and storeroom. Try not to disturb our ~~latest~~ guest, the one who thought he was a fish. Tosh and Lenny, please secure our load. We're over tonnage by the books, but our sweet girl *Becky's Pride* has gone through much worse, and we're still here. Witboy, these waters are legendary for salmon and halibut. Drop some lines and catch us some dinner as we go by! My sweet wife, join me in the cockpit to help us stay on course?" Grandpa said.

"Of course, Grandpa!" chimed his granddaughters. The blind fisherman quietly smiled. For as many wicked men were out there, there were just as many good, honest folk to balance them. He was just lucky to have such a wonderful family.

Henry woke in a strange place under a pile of wool blankets to the unique rhythmic motion fishing boats have in six-meter waves. What woke him wasn't the clang of a dropped skillet, it was a little girl's voice, quickly hushed. He sat up.

"We're sorry we woke you," said the older girl's voice. Henry shook his head and focused on the girls. They were expertly putting away cookware from breakfast in cabinets as they looked at Henry curiously. They looked like sisters, with their pale straw hair. The younger one glanced guiltily away; it was obvious who exactly the 'we' was that dropped a pan.

She was Lily's age and his heart rose in his throat.

"I wasn't really sleeping, so it doesn't matter how much noise you make," Henry said a little hoarsely. The sisters quickly exchanged a mischievous look, and the noise level rose considerably. He laughed without thinking, and so did they. Then his memories crashed back down on his head. He felt guilty for laughing, as if this was somehow a betrayal of his family, but he let nothing of this show on his face. He nodded politely.

"My name is Henry," he said.

"I'm Carlotta and this is my little sister, Emily," said the older of the two.

"Can I help?" he asked. Emily giggled.

"You're our guest, Mr. Henry. Grandma would kill me!" laughed Carlotta.

"Or make you sew up the holes in everyone's socks," suggested Emily, and Carlotta looked horrified at the thought. Henry chuckled and laid back down. Then the dark of dream wrapped its arms around him and pulled Henry down to a place where everyone he loved was still alive.

"Witboy, come inside," Grandpa ordered from the door of the cockpit. The wind almost drowned out his voice, but the boy pulled up his last line, secured his fishing gear in a storage locker and dragged two huge halibut of at least ten kilos each into the close quarters of the pilot house. Grandma chuckled and hefted one. It took both arms, but Grandma was pretty tough for an old lady.

"This will feed us for days! Good job Witboy!" she exclaimed. Witboy blushed at the praise and turned to face the helm, where the blind fisherman expertly steered them past Neah Bay, around the northwestern tip of Washington, and into the choppy waters of the Pacific Ocean.

Chapter 35

Armory Twenty-Two

The Navy special forces were grimly determined. They had almost lost one of their own, and despite the finely-tuned situational awareness of such highly trained men and women, they had never seen it coming. Tigerkind were incredibly fast and smart, too. That was something no one could've seen coming! But that was okay; SEALs are unorthodox warriors themselves. Next time they were going to be ready, because they'd just finished going through Armory Twenty-two and had acquired what they needed. Some of the weapons were almost too large for a man to wield, but they weren't just any men; they were SEALs.

And these weren't just any weapons, either.

Marc opened the coffin-sized arms case and smiled. He had found the only successful Navy attempt to produce a rail gun that could be wielded by a single person. Until this weapon, all the previous prototypes took up an entire destroyer's forward deck.

The rail gun weighed a little over ninety kilos, including the battery backpack, and the gun was as long as Marc was tall, but that's not saying much. The SEAL team leader silently thanked the brainiacs down in the basement who'd dreamed up this proto-type weapon of awesome destruction. He couldn't wait to fire it, but first he needed to get back to base.

By dawn, the techs had launched sentry drones with IR cameras that would show any heat signatures larger than a rabbit. Then the teams methodically shut down the outlying guard posts and regrouped in the main operations bunker. Every man and woman remaining on the base was there. Everyone had the discipline not to show any excitement, but inside their heads they shredded the Tigers with their bare hands. Nobody, Tiger or human, was going to take Kitsap-Bangor this day. Before this day was over, everyone would be tested beyond what they had ever been trained for.

By eleven-hundred, the heavy lifting weaponry was in position and in the process of being sighted in. The killing fields were laid out and ready. All they needed to do was wait for dark and the Tigers' return. Nobody had any doubt they were coming.

When nightfall's robes of black came sweeping over the land, the Tigers came with the darkness. Major Malgato had decided on a three-pronged attack, with her team leading from the established forward base, Ziming's squad would circle around to the back of the building, and the Yu-Kui's squad would perform a front door surgical strike. It was a good plan for a low-tech enemy who was dug in and hiding, but the Navy SEALs of Kitsap-Bangor were neither low-tech nor sailors who hide in holes, unless it was for strategic reasons.

Tigers took pride in their stealth abilities and were normally quite good at sneaking up on their prey. They also had additional spectrum bandwidth built into their heavily enhanced vision. But the Peoples Republic had long since discarded IR heat vision as antiquated tech, so this night the Tigers were completely unaware of their glowing hot footprint. They didn't expect to be seen until it was too late. Tigers were all about the initial blitz attack.

"Squad Leader Ziming. The humans have abandoned their outlying nests. All indications are that they scurried back to the main nest through underground tunnels. Have located a suspected ammo vault; I can smell the nitrates and gel explosives from here. Big heavy door; we'll need at least five minutes to get in. *Hhuff.*" the Tiger squad leader announced.

"Major. Focus on the vault. We need to dig these rodents out and explosives are just the right shovel. Maintain vigilance," Major Malgato ordered. Turning to the third squad leader, she hissed, "Squad Leader Yu-Kui, report!"

"Commander, Humans have locked down everything and retreated through a well-sealed tunnel. Estimate twenty minutes to burn our way into the passage," the Tiger reported.

"Acceptable. Report in ten minutes. You should be halfway done by then. *Hhuff,*" the major suggested with just a hint of snarl.

"Squad Leader Ziming. We're in. Huge place. Stuffed full of explosives. Send additional Tigers to load up. We're going to blow this place into the past. *Hhuff,*" he reported.

"Good job, Ziming! Teams One and Two, rotate through the armory and stock up. Team Three, stay on task. Go!" the Major ordered.

"We are about four minutes from your position. Wait until I get there before you enter the tunnel," the major demanded of Squad Leader Yu-Kui. "It's sure to be loaded with counter-measures, so just..." the Major said, as someone on the other end of the headset roared in triumph.

"Don't worry, I can't smell any sign of explosives, just going to take a peek...".

This was immediately followed by the percussive howl of a ship's main Gatling guns. In the confined space of the tunnel the sheer decibels of the death metal were enough to destroy a Tiger's hearing. It didn't really matter; the hurricane of depleted-uranium projectiles at over three thousand rounds a minute didn't leave any traces of the unfortunate Tiger. Even with intravenous nanites, there was no coming back from that.

The Major spit angrily. What a waste! But Ten Tigers were still enough to conquer a nation, much less to clean out a nest of vermin and stake territory in the new land. She turned back to face the human garrison and lifted her sniper rifle to examine its walls again.

Too much concertina razor-wire covering all of the first story of the hardened building. The second story had heavy steel shutters over the few windows on this side and only three meters of tangled barbwire instead of four meters like below. Trying to go through that would be like swimming in razor-sharp water. They would heal quickly, but it would be distracting for her team at a time when focus was crucial for survival. But a few quick burrows under the concertina wire, to specific targets would be possible.

She studied what she could see of the roof. It contained a significant number of perches for snipers, and several things concealed behind three large barricades. Maybe something that could lob shells without exposing itself to return fire. Possibly loaded with anti-personnel frag bomblets that scatter before going off.

Malgato turned to her third officer and flicked a claw at their field mortar.

"Prepare for firing, let's do some housecleaning on the top floor. Front to back, incendiary mortars mixed with demolition shells. When I give the order, I want you to level the building top-down. Leave some nice big holes that we can follow down into the nest and exterminate the remaining humans," Major Malgato ordered.

She turned back to the target, focusing with one eye through the scope.

"Stealth attack up to the wall, under the razor wire, plant explosives and get back to cover. I will give the signal. Then you blow the walls. Leave your rifles here; they'll catch in the wire. You'll be close enough that machine pistols and scatterguns will perform better anyway," Major Malgato ordered. "Go!" she hissed. The major turned to her mortar Tiger. "Fire!" she said.

The first shell was incendiary and was very bright as it ignited in a brilliant fire that engulfed the roof before blowing it clean of everything concealed on it. Flaming debris fell, surreal and scarlet in the night. The burning pieces landed almost gently in the tall grass, spreading flames, rendering the bunker's heat-vision drones useless.

The second shell blew a hole the size of an elephant in the third-story floor. Those that followed progressively drilled down through the concrete and rebar and took out the interior sections of the building they were collapsing. Then the explosive shells hit the floor over the roof to the hardened underground command center and stopped making progress.

The Major's men were just digging their way under the razor-sharp spread of barbed wire when concealed blinds low in the wall opened and somebody started shooting her Tigers.

This was annoying, because her Tigers were trapped in the shallow trenches they were digging under the razor wire. Her sappers kept on mission and shrugged off the swarming bullets as they continued to dig forward. Those few expended projectiles that made it past their body armor were already being pushed back out of their healing flesh. A few seconds later, when the Tigers were almost to the wall, the enemy switched tactics and began firing grenades at them.

Those were harder to shrug off.

When they had come within a single meter from the wall, one of the grenades prematurely set off the explosives they'd loyally dragged behind them. The fireball was so bright it made the Major's eyes involuntarily close. She didn't need to open them to know that she'd just lost two of her team, vaporized into dust.

Suddenly her Tiger-senses went off and she spun to face whatever was behind her.

Twenty meters away without any readable emotion, Marc stepped out from the shadow of a parked transport truck, staring directly at her. He was powerfully built for a human and steadied some kind of strange weapon on his right shoulder. Then he aimed it slightly to the Major's left side, where the mortar and its operator crouched. The violent crack of the rail gun firing was slower than the half-meter hole in her Tiger's chest that was torn open and gone. The second shot was instantaneous as well but lower, leaving the Tiger operating the mortar without a mortar or lower body. The Major had just lost another team member. The SEAL staggered back under the mule-kick of the gun as the weapon recharged. Major Malgato took advantage of this to place two heavy slugs in the SEAL's chest and he fell the rest of the way to the ground. After a moment he sat up, shook his head once and rolled back up to its feet, taking aim at the Major herself.

She wasn't the only one wearing armor.

As before, the report hurt her ears and the vacuum created by the metallic projectiles passing clapped loudly as air rushed in to replace the emptiness. Major Malgato screeched in rage as she threw herself to the side, even though they both knew there was no dodging this weapon. That was when another Tiger took the Navy man in a leap that left both of them on the ground and the strange gun broken on the grass. Then the Tiger seemed to levitate above the human for a second before it fell to the side, but in reality, it was just catching repeated shotgun blasts from the human. The Major was deaf for the moment and hadn't heard anything.

This was not going well at all.

"Regroup by the water!" she ordered curtly by headset, but she was unable to hear any acknowledgment, so the Major didn't know if anyone received it. Then a damned Navy missile launcher let loose across the grass and debris, and several anti-tank missiles blew two of her Tigers into a red fog. "Move!" she growled and took her own advice.

They didn't stop until they hit the Hood Canal.

Chapter 36

Bear Town

We were silent as we sneaked around the half-circle of the small town, watching for any sign of life. When we found a sign of life, it walked on all fours and was fat. Hungry, too.

None of us could remember seeing such a creature. I turned my head back to sniff Rachel's hair and give a questioning look. She smiled brightly and leaned forward to whisper in my ear; we were quiet-walking, and she knew she should be as silent as possible.

"It's a bear! There are good bears that eat porridge and dance. But there are also bad bears that attack people. I think that's a bad bear," Rachel whispered very quietly. I nodded in agreement and crept closer through the overgrown plants of an untended garden. It was beautiful if you liked plants. All I saw were a lot of caged plants finally breaking free of man's chains and shackles, and that was beautiful to me. I sighed and eased to a stop at the gate to the street and peeked over the puny stone wall to study the bear.

It sat leaning against the storefront of a little grocery store with broken windows. The bear was massive, with rough brownish fur that was stained crimson on its chest.

177

Fangs almost as big as the Tigers', set in an impressive set of jaws, and powerful legs tipped with long black claws. Its black eyes roamed his surroundings casually, confident that it was the baddest beast in the forest. His right paw was resting on a broken ribcage that looked human.

Rachel was right; it was one of the bad ones.

But it was also quite fat, and all that bulk probably took a while to get moving. The bear wouldn't be able to change directions quickly with all that mass, and we Wolves excelled at that. But if that thing got its claws in one of us, it was going to be terrible.

"Five, Two, Thirteen and Four, dash by and slice him up. Hamstring him. Be very fast—I'm not losing anyone else now. Go!" I ordered under my breath. I knew my pack would hear me, but I didn't realize bears have very good hearing as well. This time something big and smelly peeked back at me when I returned my gaze to the bear.

I was right; all that belly took a while to get moving. But I hadn't realized just how powerful this beast was. In a blink, it was to the gate and crashing through it without a pause. Part of the gate hung on its neck for several steps. It bounded forward, roaring louder than I could remember ever hearing.

I was shocked. It would be on me when it landed!

I spun to my left and took off like hell was chasing me—because it was. The bear was so close behind me I could smell its rancid breath. I guess I was wrong about the bear's ability to change direction, because the next time I dodged right an ebony claw raked my back on the left side. It took part of me with it, but my nanites were already busy repairing the tissue and bone. Hurt like hell.

Meanwhile, Two and Six took out its leg tendon and the enormous bear sagged on its right rear leg as it lost the ability to support its body. I spun on my paws and turned to face the bear. Five took out its left front leg without taking any damage. The bear roared its volcanic anger and swiped at us with its remaining paw, even though it had to realize we were out of reach. We gathered around it at a safe distance and were silent before its magnificent rage.

"We can't leave it like this; it could suffer for weeks before it dies. We're not cruel," I quietly stated. Then I had Rachel get down and join Eleven and Bookworm. I looked around. The pack was of one mind. I took my shotgun off my back and reloaded it with solid slugs. I stepped to the massive bear's side, just out of reach. It watched me with hating eyes, knowing what came next. I jacked a slug into the shotgun's chamber and blew its brains out. Then I stepped back, looking at the fallen enemy's body.

"We should cut off its skin and make a blanket like the pioneers did," Bookworm said quietly. His voice was a little rough from disuse and he shyly looked at the ground instead of us.

I didn't look stunned or make a big deal about hearing his voice for the first time like some humans might. I just nodded at him.

"Good idea, Bookworm. Five? We should save the meat, too. That's a lot of bear steaks. Now, who wants to go shopping?" I said. My mancub was healing. I felt happiness but didn't let my tail wag.

We left Nine, Twelve, Two and Six to butcher the meat into pieces small enough to carry. They saved the skin too, taking time to shave the fat layer off but leaving the fur intact.

"Time to resupply. The cubs need more vitamins. We need to gather supplies for building our new home—shovels, axes, hammers, and nails. Remember the vid with a single human making a log cabin with that little hand axe? Make sure to get enough of those. Five take point. One, Four, Eight, and Thirteen - we don't want to get taken by surprise. You're on lookout. Go!" I ordered my Wolves. Rachel wiggled and spoke with a warm breath.

"Can we go shopping now and get some candy?" she asked.

"Just candy?" I replied as I crossed the broken glass to enter the store behind Nine.

"Uh… vitamins, protein, and SpaghettiOs?" she replied tentatively. I nuzzled her hair and then ducked to avoid a low light fixture.

"Yes, we are all going shopping," I said. She beamed so strongly that I could feel it on the back of my neck. Well, I could also see it with the small piece of mirror tucked into the wrist cuff of my long-coat. I had a lot to learn about human expressions, and this helped. It also made me feel good when I could see she was happy.

Forty minutes later we were fully refitted and leaving town for the mountains to the west. We had also stocked up on fruit snacks and gummy bears at the cub's insistence. As we were leaving, we found a bunch of little yellow pine houses perched out over the water. Each had a door with a number on it. The roofs were very sharply angled, and I wondered aloud why the humans thought this was good. They were all empty of life, but we found discarded fishing stuff, heavy coats, and even a few bulky computers. Eleven's eyes lit up at those, and they quickly vanished into her backpack. Everyone found a heavy coat and warm hat that would fit them. The cubs had lots of choices, and it took a while for them to choose their favorites. We didn't get a chance to give them special things very often.

The nights were getting cold, but we still had a three-quarter moon to see by. We found a trail that humans had improved and made good time. We needed to be in the rainforest before the winter snows came down out of the mountains.

"Eleven, pull up that map you have on the computer. I want us to be at our new home before the snows hit. Everyone, gather around. Bookworm, please pass around the water," I said, calling a halt before we descended into the next valley.

"See here? That thin line in brown is this trail," Eleven explained. Some Wolves got it right away, some didn't. The line on the screen didn't look like anything at all to most of us.

"Our satellite GPS shows us here," she said, pointing. The Hoh Rain Forest was just two mountains away. I yipped in excitement, and everyone got into the act. We were almost home!

"That's the good news. The bad news is we'll have to go around the big mountains, because it's too cold and the mountains are too high to go over," she explained. "We'll have to go through Forks on our way." She waited for us to get it.

"Forks? That's where those sparkly vampires live; remember those awful documentaries on YouTube?" I growled. Everyone growled in agreement.

"I don't think we should take such a long route. Why can't we just go over the mountain? See that high mountain pass?" I asked, pointing a talon at the map. Eleven respectfully steered my paw away from the screen.

"The screens scratch easily, and then we can't see as well," she explained quietly. "We've already damaged three computer screens too much to use. We need to be careful," she added.

I noticed the pack was watching me intently to see how I dealt with this minor interference with my movement. Alphas have to notice the nuances of their pack to be good leaders. Bad leaders don't last.

"Eleven, make sure everybody knows how to safely touch the computers. I don't want to go through Forks. Let's go that way," I said, pointing up into the mountains from a safe distance. Eleven just nodded and pointed further across the valley and up.

"I think we can go up over that, up to the place trees can't grow, where all the snow is. We're going to need sunglasses if we move during the day," she said. Lots of tail wagging.

Of course, we didn't know what we were getting into.

Chapter 37

A Mutiny of Tigers

"To hell with these humans—both Chinese and barbarian; we are Tigers and tower above their machinations," snarled Major Malgato. Her remaining team of five stood silent, their nanites working overtime to heal their gaping wounds and expel shrapnel. She was so disgusted she could spit, so she did spit, as only a Tiger can.

Things hadn't gone well at Kitsap-Bangor.

Now her superiors had ordered her to report in person to the fleet commander onboard the PLAN Attack Carrier anchored in Vancouver harbor. She was expected to explain how she not only failed to take an almost undefended Trident base, but somehow managed to lose over half of her very-expensive team of Tigers at the same time!

This was the kind of order that, at best, meant back to the mind-wipe-trials, and, at worst, a bullet in the back of her head. This was no mere matter of speech; there was a deliberate flaw built into her genetically re-engineered Tiger body. It was a failsafe for humans to utilize should they lose control of their creations. A bullet in the right spot fired at the proper upwards angle to the back of her head was enough to retire even the Major. But she wasn't going to let it come to that. The time when Tigers answered to mice was over.

She shook her head to clear it but shaking her head didn't help. She glared at her team and finally spoke.

"We are done following the orders of humans. They've sent us to our deaths for the last time. We're going to the mountains we saw on the western side of this mountain range. We're going to live as we've only dreamed of. We're going to stake a large territory with a mountain for every Tiger and defend our mountain tops from mice and machines. Those damned Dogs, too. Our home will be a place where Tigers can finally roam free through their own lands and hunt as they choose," said the Major. She scornfully turned her back on the burning remnants of Kitsap-Bangor Trident base and its surviving human defenders, those damn SEALs. Major Malgato flicked her tail in an insulting manner at the thought and began retracing her steps back to those mountains they'd admired soon after arriving on the Olympic Peninsula.

Maybe they'd even run across another elk herd on their way.

Chapter 38

The Redoubt

It was the wind that I noticed first. A slicing blow that robbed a body of heat if you let it. We were ten minutes past the mountain's tree line, about two-and-a-half thousand meters above sea level. We forged a trail in an almost straight line through knee-high brush well dusted with ice and snow. A sullen half-moon hung above the horizon lending little light and no heat to the sterile air. I thought this place was scent dead at first. Then we began noticing small differences in things we'd previously lumped under 'snow'. The minute differences began to correlate to the ground under our paws. Eventually we were able to smell the ground and know which way the safer ice lay. Until we were in a scent desert, we had no idea what our noses were capable of.

"Are you cold, cub?" I asked Rachel over my shoulder. We had been marching for over five hours. She shivered and said, "No." I held in a Wolf grin.

"I always tell you the truth, daughter. Please do the same," I said in a gruff, but affectionate voice. I peered through the wind-driven snow for a place to rest. No place immediately obvious. I looked back at my cub.

"Yes, Alpha. I'm a little cold," Rachel said with a sniff. I nuzzled her hair quickly and stood tall to be heard better. The wind was louder than I had expected.

"Everyone, find a place for us to go to ground and give us all a chance to rest and get warm," I ordered. My pack spread out, and soon Twelve called everyone to her.

It was a crude redoubt, built of slate and honeycombed pumice, the cracks stuffed with well-aged straw and clay. We all fit, with room for maybe three more. There was an ancient fire pit, and a pile of old firewood next to it. Five made quick use of his fire building skills and soon the shelter began to warm up. The narrow entryway underneath the stone outcropping that sheltered us was open to the wind, but was designed so that only the occasional gust made it all the way in.

"We're going to need more fuel for the fire soon," Five said. It was a long way to the tree line for wood, but we had seen some stunted shrubs that might do.

"The pioneers burned cow and buffalo manure in the plains where there weren't any trees. I think deer and sheep dung might work as well up here," volunteered Bookworm.

"Good suggestion, cub! Wolves, try to find dried out scat instead of fresh. Rotate in pairs of two to gather fuel. Eight and Four—go first. The rest of us nap, drink water and eat some bear meat or have a protein shake. Go" I ordered. I nudged Rachel closer to the fire and handed her a few protein bars. She gravely accepted them and began to poke at the fire with a stick as she gnawed on a protein bar. I couldn't read her expression as she stared into the flames.

The wind howled like the Mongol heavy metal on YouTube, and snow began to fall. The temperature dropped rapidly, but we stayed almost warm in the ancient stone shelter with the fire. Then Bookworm suggested something to Eleven, so she unfolded the rawhide bear skin, and spread it out over our mound of sleepy Wolves. It was big enough to cover us all, and we warmed up almost immediately. Soon only Wolf noses protruded out from under the fur blanket. Pairs of Wolves rotated out through the long night on fire fuel missions, but the sun didn't come out the next day. I felt like it was the best sleep I could remember in my life. We'd been on the move for such a long time, and we were bone weary. But eventually even the most exhausted Wolf gets enough sleep. We didn't know how long the snowstorm lasted, but eventually I found I couldn't sit still any longer. I nosed my main tech Wolf, Seven.

"Seven, can you get a satellite signal from here? Need to know where we are, and how long this storm is going to last," I asked, my voice slightly muffled by the bearskin over us. She was fully awake and seemed anxious to get to work again. Then somebody farted and we all discovered the downside of sharing a bearskin blanket. Silent Wolf laughter mixed with annoyed snarls was enough to wake up anyone still sleeping.

Sometimes it's the simple things that make you smile.

The sun was infernally bright when it finally showed up, reflected a thousand times on the diamond snowfields. So, this was what Eleven had meant when she said we'd need sunglasses! I pulled out mine from an inner pocket. Good thing they were part of our normal urban disguise. I felt my squint relax as I put them on. Now I could see. I nodded to Eleven. She was already wearing hers.

I was glad that we'd learned how to truly use our noses as we hobbled along the boulder-strewn mountainside through the thick snow. We walked in a row, some of us with rags tied over our eyes to protect them, the others leading the way in our sunglasses.–We substituted scent for sight; our progress was slow but steady, and we ate up the kilometers. Then I smelled it. I had never breathed in this particular

187

mixture of damp plant and moss, of incense cedar, pine, and mushrooms gone wild, but I knew it immediately.

Home.

The Hoh Rain Forest, at last.

Three hours later, we came to a halt on a ridge overlooking the rainforest. Trees towered high and thick, dressed in lush mosses and lichen. The sheer multitude of shades of green below us was stunning. We stood silently, staring at the promised land we had traveled so long and far to find. After a moment, a dollop of breeze carried the smell of wood smoke and a faint piano music that seemed very familiar to us. I grinned and started down the ridge. Rachel whooped and dug her heels into my sides.

The rest of our pack was waiting for us down there in Wolfland.

There might even be Cioppino.

The End

***Watch for the sequel, "Bad Cat, Good Wolf"!*
Three and his pack have reached Wolfland, but now the task of surviving and defending it must be tackled. Power and towers, fighting and training, Wolves, cubs, and human allies are all needed. It's going to be a long winter.

I want to thank my editor, Diana Adamson, and publisher Suzanne Hagelin, whose hard work and patience with me have made this a far better book than it might have been. Thanks to Natasha Kennedy who captured my vision for this book and created an incredible cover. Thanks to Mark, who's offhand remark as we drove past Indian Island after an evening of Thai food and local beer in Port Townsend created Three and his pack.

And thanks to my father, who introduced me to science fiction long ago.

—Eric

About the Author

Eric Little lives in the Pacific Northwest, drawn by his love of the mountains and rainforests. He slings wine by day and writes science fiction by night. He has a lifelong background in the martial arts with Sun Tai Chi, Lu Bagua, and Xing-Yi being his preferred styles. Eric has two sci-fi series in process at this time and has published short stories in the 2018 and 2019 NIWA anthologies, "Carnival" and "Doorways".

The Summer War Cycle: The first book, "Summerlight" is available and the prequel, "Summerstead" is in the editing stages. Two more books, "Summertime" and "Summerwar" will complete the cycle.

Bad Dog, Good Wolf: The sequel, "Bad Cat, Good Wolf" will be out soon, followed by "Bad Bear, Good Wolf".

Follow Eric on Twitter: @Yipman44

www.ingramcontent.com/pod-product-compliance
Lightning Source LLC
Chambersburg PA
CBHW071156180726
48291CB00007B/2480